THE MAN FROM
SANTA ROSA

THE MAN FROM SANTA ROSA

by

Tom Benson

Dales Large Print Books
Long Preston, North Yorkshire,
BD23 4ND, England.

British Library Cataloguing in Publication Data.

Benson, Tom
     The man from Santa Rosa.

     A catalogue record of this book is
     available from the British Library

     ISBN   1-84262-332-X pbk

First published in Great Britain 2003 by Robert Hale Ltd.

Copyright © Tom Benson 2003

Cover illustration © Lopez by arrangement with
Norma Editorial S.A.

Published in Large Print 2004 by arrangement with
Robert Hale Ltd.

Dales Large Print is an imprint of Library Magna Books Ltd.

Printed and bound in Great Britain by
T.J. (International) Ltd., Cornwall, PL28 8RW

ONE

The sun was setting low behind the distant hills and the rumbling carriage threw long shadows over the trail. It was a black vehicle, four-wheeled, and with slender painted spokes that had gilded stripes like some town gig. There was a thick coating of dust all over it, and the two horses, almost black when they set out from Tucson, were now a reddish mess of streaks as they careered across the uneven ground.

It was a closed rig, finely made, and driven by a large man whose broad hat was low over his reddened face. He was covered in dust as was the guard who sat beside him with a shotgun across his knees. A long cloud lay to mark their trail, hovering in the still air to settle over the sparse grass and clumps of mesquite along the route.

They came to a rocky gulch that threw up long slopes of jagged stone striped red and various shades of yellow in the failing daylight. The trail narrowed to wend its way through the gap of what had once been a watercourse. The driver pulled in the horses a little to slow them down among the small bits of fallen rock that dotted the trail to shake the delicate wheels which should never have been seen outside the comforts of Tucson. The carriage rocked on its springs as it negotiated the almost canyon-like passage which blotted out the last of the setting sun.

It was just as they reached the end of the gulch that the first shot was fired. It took the driver high in the chest and he slipped back on his seat before pitching off the rig and falling against the reddish rocks at the side of the trail. He let out a yell as his body bounced off a ledge and slipped behind the carriage.

The guard muttered a curse and dropped the shotgun as he tried to seize the falling reins. He missed them as they slapped down between the two horses while he had to grab hurriedly for the Colt at his side.

Another shot split the air and he lurched in his seat before collapsing across its length. His body bounced on the sprung boards and then pitched forward to slide against the brake lever. The horses had increased speed at the sound of the gunfire and the rig swayed sickeningly as it pitched over the rocky trail. There were shrieks from inside the carriage in the high voices of terrified women.

A lone horseman sat on a small roan mare about fifty feet ahead of the rig. He was a short, dark man with an impassive face who waited patiently for the team to come level. He reached out and grabbed the bridle of the animal nearest to him. It struggled and tried to rear against the sudden pain. He held on with a strong hand, controlling his own mount with ease as he gradually drew the carriage horses to a halt.

The air was full of dust, and steam rose

from the animals as everything fell suddenly silent in the narrow trail between the low walls of rock.

Four more men appeared from their hiding-places. They were on foot and carried Winchesters. All of them were grinning broadly as they ran towards the doors of the rig and flung them open to see who was being driven in such a fine town carriage.

The shot took them by surprise and one man staggered backwards with an agonized cry on his lips as he rolled in the dirt with blood oozing out of his chest. One of the others reached into the carriage and fired a couple of shots from his Winchester. There was a high-pitched scream, another explosion from the depths of the rig, and then a sudden silence broken only by the rattle of the Winchester cartridge cases as they rolled over the pebbles.

The lone rider had quietened the two carriage horses and was able to dismount from his own animal. He walked with a slight limp as he came round to the open door of the rig to look inside. He did not even bother to glance at the man who had been shot by one of the occupants.

There were two women in the carriage. They sat facing each other, lolling back in their seats without movement. Both had been shot dead and one still had a four-barrelled derringer lying on her lap. She was a woman in her fifties, well dressed and with gold jewellery on her fingers and round her neck. The other woman was younger. She was a black girl, neatly dressed and obviously a ladies' maid.

'You didn't have to shoot them,' the leader said quietly. 'It ain't a good thing to kill women.'

'That old bitch shot Ted,' one of the men protested. 'She had two more bullets in that thing so I had to do something.'

The boss nodded sadly. 'I guess so,' he conceded. 'Right, let's get the stuff we want and head outa here.'

The men began unpacking the luggage

that littered the carriage. They tore open leather cases and carpetbags in their frenzied search. While they worked, the wounded man lay at the side of the track, bleeding from his chest injury and pleading with his comrades to help him. Nobody took any notice as they ransacked the interior of the rig.

'It ain't here, Walt,' one of the men complained as he flung an empty carpetbag on to the ground. 'They ain't got it with them.'

'She could be carryin' it,' their boss said impatiently. 'Search her.'

The other bandits looked at each other and then at the body of the woman. They seemed a little squeamish at laying hands on a corpse. Walt gave a snort of disgust and pushed them aside. He bent over the body, his hands moving swiftly across the smooth cotton of the store-bought frock. He let out a sudden yell of triumph as one of his hands came away with a small, paper-wrapped packet that the woman had been hiding in a pocket built into the folds of her skirt.

'Now let's get the hell outa here!' he shouted. He jumped down from the rig and headed for his horse.

The other men grabbed what jewellery they could see and began to follow him. One of them glanced at their injured companion who was now moaning softly.

'What about Ted?' he asked. 'We can't leave him here.'

Their leader stopped in his tracks.

'You've got the right of it there, fella,' he said after a slight pause. He went to the injured man and looked down at him.

'You're hurt bad, Ted,' he said calmly, 'and we can't take you to no doctor. Then again, we can't leave you here to talk to any sheriff or marshal who happens to pass by.'

He pulled the .44 from his belt and shot the man in the head. The others watched with uneasy expressions on their greedy faces.

'Now unhitch those horses,' the killer ordered crisply, 'and then let's move out.

We're finished here.'

The stage to Fort Grant made the journey every Thursday. It rattled through the haze of sandy grit with the four mules trailing yards of white foam from their sweating mouths. It carried the mails, a few passengers, and all the latest gossip from the big cities. The driver was hunched over the reins while the guard sat with a rifle across his knee as he chewed tobacco and spat occasionally with the expertise of long practice.

They reached the gulch at just about noon and saw the carriage that lay derelict across the trail. It was thick with dust, and buzzards rose from the ground at the approach of the stage. The driver pulled at the reins while his partner levelled the Winchester uneasily as he stared around in case an ambush had been set.

'I reckon as how this happened a few days ago,' he muttered with a sigh of relief. 'I'll go take a look. Keep me covered, fella.'

Passengers were leaning out of the windows in an effort to see what was happening while the guard climbed down from his high perch and approached the rig with a certain caution. He saw the body of the dead bandit lying at the side of the trail and noticed that while one shot was a chest wound, the other was a neat one in the centre of the head. It had been fired at close range and the wound was tattooed with burned powder.

There was another body at the other side of the rig. It had been partly eaten by scavengers and he took it to be the driver or guard of the carriage. Another corpse was still lying below the driver's seat and had obviously been attacked by the buzzards. The stage guard looked in at the open door. There were two women there, dead and pale in the dim light. He turned back to the stage and reported to the driver.

'It's some fancy town rig,' he said dubiously. 'Two women dead inside it and the driver and guard both shot. All their baggage has been searched and anythin' worth while has been taken. What do we do, Eddy? We can't leave the bodies here.'

The driver climbed down to join the three passengers who were now stretching their legs and brushing dust off their clothes.

'We can't take 'em aboard the stage either,' he said quietly. 'These folks will yell somethin' terrible if they have to share with dead bodies. We'll just report to the marshal at Fort Grant and let him worry. I reckon we'd better move on as soon as we can drag that rig outa the way. We'll put the other bodies inside it and close the doors. That'll keep the buzzards away until the marshal gets here. Best get moving.'

The three passengers were men who were used to rough travel and they willingly lent their muscle to move the rig along the trail until it widened enough to let their own bulky stagecoach get past.

It was when they started shifting the dead bodies that one of the passengers let out a yell of surprise.

'These fellas is soldier-boys!' he said excitedly. 'This one's a sergeant.'

The others gathered round and could see that as the body was disturbed by being lifted, the dust had fallen away and the yellow stripes on the arm came clearly into view.

They all stood looking at the corpses in silence for a few moments before picking them up and moving them across to the carriage. It was the same passenger who gave vent to another grunt of surprise. He leaned forward to get a better look at the face of the older woman in the dimness of the rig.

'I know her,' he murmured in a subdued voice. 'It's Colonel Barstin's wife.'

TWO

The man who drove the buckboard was feeling contented. He had just done some good deals in Tucson and was on his way home to Santa Rosa with the certain knowledge that he was going to make some fine profits from his work. He was a big man, fat and well groomed, with a neat moustache and keen grey eyes that were surrounded by healthy and well-shaven flesh. His clothes were from a large town, covered now by a white trail coat and a fine layer of dust, but showing their quality to any close observer.

Jesse Clark was a successful businessman and everybody in his home town paid him the respect due to wealth and power. He drove the rig with a light hand, guiding the horse gently at a steady clip that would get him into Santa Rosa by nightfall.

He had travelled a long way in the last couple of days. His food was nearly exhausted but he would dine tonight at his own ample table, and then take a stroll along to the saloon he owned to see how things were going. Jesse smiled to himself as he watched the distant hills to see the sun drawing closer to the dark blue of the peaks. Two more hours at a steady pace and he would be in his own domain.

He heard the laughter before he rounded the bend to turn into a slight dip in the trail.

There were three horses tethered together amid a clump of mesquite, while their riders stood in a group below a sprawling sycamore at the side of the track. They turned as he approached and he realized that there was a fourth man who had a rope around his neck. It was a lynching party.

Jesse hauled at the reins and his rig came to a halt just a few yards away from the little group. He took in the scene with shrewd appraisal. It was a young black man they

19

were hanging, and the executioners were enjoying the festive occasion. One of them had already thrown the rope over a branch but stopped to see what the driver of the buckboard wanted.

'Having fun, fellas?' Jesse asked in his rich, jovial voice.

One of the three came to stand at the head of the fat man's horse.

'Just hangin' ourselves a thief,' he said with a wide grin on his unshaven face.

Jesse Clark nodded. 'Well, hanging a thief can't be such a bad thing. There's many a thief I'd have liked to hang in my day. What did he steal?'

'Chickens,' one of the others said as he spat out a wad of tobacco. 'Took half a dozen of my best layers, he did. We tracked him down to a camp he'd made just behind them rocks. And there he was, gettin' all set to cook one of them.'

Jesse clicked his tongue sadly. 'You can't trust anybody these days,' he said. 'Do you reckon he might have been hungry?'

The question took them all by surprise, and even the prisoner raised his bruised head at such a question.

'Hungry?' The fellow who stood closest to Jesse Clark looked up at the fat man as though he were mad.

'Well, folks do get hungry once in a while,' Jesse said quietly, 'and the Good Book tells us somethin' about showing Christian charity.'

The three men looked at each other and their grins widened.

'A fella can always work to get food,' one of them ventured while the others nodded their heads in agreement.

'It could be a bit hard for a black man to get honest work around here,' Jesse Clark said. There was a slight change in his voice but the others did not notice it. 'Let him go.'

The man by the horse stopped grinning.

'Let him go?' he echoed. 'You think we should turn this fella loose to go robbin' other decent folk? Hell, you'd better be on your way afore we hangs you with him. We got enough rope for it.'

'You've already given him a hiding and scared him to hell and back. Now, let him go.'

The fellow by the horse turned to look at his friends.

'This fat man sure has a mouth full of words,' he sneered. 'I reckon as how we could use this buckboard that he's spoutin' from. Get down from that rig, fella, afore I forgets my manners and puts a bullet in your hide.'

He reached out with his left hand and grabbed the horse's noseband just above the bit. His other hand was hovering over the butt of a Remington at his side. Jesse Clark did not move.

'Make me,' he said in a thin voice.

The three men burst out laughing, and one of them came over to the buckboard to get a closer look.

'He's sure one brave man,' he shouted to the others. 'Ain't wearin' a gun and with an old carbine under the seat where he can't even reach it. You'd better do what Clint tells you, fat man. He kinda likes shootin' folks, and he ain't goin' to miss a big target like you.'

Jesse looked down at the speaker. His voice had the quality of a knife-blade as he spoke, but the men were too careless to notice it.

'I don't reckon the three of you put together would frighten a half-dead jack-rabbit,' he said. 'Who wants to die first?'

It took a moment for his words to really sink in. The one who held the bridle was the first to react. He reached down for the gun at his side and a shot cut through the dusk with a suddenness that silenced the birds and made the horses shake their heads in fear.

Jesse Clark was still seated on the buckboard. A Colt .44 was in his right hand, recocked and pointing at the one who had come to check on whether or not the fat man was carrying a gun. The fellow's face was a study in terror. He found himself staring at a weapon that had appeared like magic from beneath the white trail coat that Jesse wore over his clothes. He looked at his companion who had been holding the horse's head. The man had been killed before his pistol even left the holster.

The third man was the first to make a move. He began to run, without as much as a backward glance to where their horses were tethered. Jesse smiled, took careful aim, and shot him cleanly through the back. The man fell in his tracks and rolled over a few times before lying still.

'And that just leaves you,' the fat man said in a gentle voice. 'Go and untie our friend there. He must be very uncomfortable by now.'

The frightened man nodded dumbly and went to carry out the order. His trembling fingers fumbled with the knot but he eventually freed the black man and then stood undecidedly as he glanced first at Jesse and then at the horses. The freed prisoner rubbed his wrists to try and restore the circulation.

'Unbuckle your gunbelt and drop it,' Jesse told the other man. 'Then you can start walking home.'

'My horse...'

'I said that you walk. Get moving before I change my mind.'

The gunbelt clattered to the ground and the man went off towards the east, glancing back occasionally as if he could not be sure of his good luck. Jesse motioned the black man to come over to the rig.

'What do they call you?' he asked as he holstered the gun.

'Abraham.' The young man's voice was cautious and polite.

Jesse smiled. 'After Abe Lincoln, I'll wager,' he mused. 'Well, that's not a popular name in this part of the world. I'll call you Sam. It's less trouble. Now, Sam, just unsaddle those horses, bring the harness over to my rig, and then collect the guns from those two dead 'uns. You might like to put on one of the belts yourself.'

He looked quizzically at the young man as he spoke.

'No, thanks, boss. I ain't wearin' no gunbelt. Us black folks have enough trouble just bein' around.'

Jesse nodded. 'I see your point. So it's one extra for me. When you've unsaddled the horses, turn 'em loose. They'll find their own way home.'

He waited patiently while the man did as he was ordered. He was a lithe young fellow, tall, slim, and dressed in wool shirt and canvas pants that were clean but worn. Jesse Clark took out a thin cigar and lit it while he waited for the saddles and guns to be piled behind him on the rig. It was all extra profit and made the day worth while. He did not want the horses. They would have brands on them.

'I'm heading for Santa Rosa,' he said when the work was done. 'You can ride with me as far as you like. Or you can go your own way.'

'Firstly, I want to thank you, boss,' the young man said with a certain dignity. 'The buzzards would be after me by now if you hadn't happened along.'

'True enough, but I had my fun and made a profit. Are you looking for work?'

'Yes, boss, and I'm a hard worker. And honest.'

'A fella who steals chickens just because he's hungry?'

The black man grinned. 'I'm still hungry, boss,' he said. 'They came along before I could finish cooking.'

Jesse laughed; a deep rumbling sound that shook his large belly.

'Climb aboard then,' he said. 'There's some bread and a bit of bacon back there, and a jug of corn mash. A man who was so near to a hanging could surely use a drink.'

The young man climbed aboard the rig and searched among the saddles and other items until he found the food. Jesse whipped up the horse and drove off at a steady pace into the fast-gathering dusk.

'We'll be in Santa Rosa by ten or eleven,' he called over his shoulder. 'There might be work for you there. Folk ain't as fussy so near the border. We got Indians, Mexicans, a couple of Chinamen, and all sorts of odd folk from Europe. When you've finished that food, come sit by me. We can talk better that way.'

They were soon side by side on the wooden seat as the buckboard clattered its way through the darkening evening towards Santa Rosa. They talked easily once the black man was certain that he was being treated like a human being and not some son of slave parents.

'I might have a job for you, Sam,' Jesse said after a while. 'Interested?'

The young man smiled in the darkness. 'I sure am, boss. What have you got in mind?'

'Well, I'm not one of the good Christian folk in Santa Rosa. I don't go to church, sing hymns, or pay heed to the Ten Commandments. In fact, I'm the crookedest man in town.'

He burst out laughing and the seat rocked on its springs.

'So my wife walked out on me one fine day, and took my two boys with her. Went back to her own folks where they could be raised properly in respectable Christian poverty. Now, I don't believe in poverty, Sam. I like to make me a dollar or two. And I don't much care how it's done.'

'And is you a rich man, boss?'

'Richest you're like to come across in this part of the world. The trouble is, there ain't many people that a man in my position can trust. Now you and me has a lot in common. Good Christian folk have a dislike of both of us. You because you're black, and me because I'm rich and dishonest. I need a man to drive this rig, look after my house, and to see what goes on but having the wit to keep his mouth shut. I have a woman comes in to clean, but women talk, and I can't have that. Interested?'

There was a moment of silence and then the young man nodded his head.

'Yes, boss. I'm interested.'

'Good. I pay a fair wage and you'll never

go hungry. There's a shed at the back of my place that's dry and clean. I'll put in a bed for you and get you some decent clothes. There's just one thing I ask of you, Sam.'

Jesse Clark stopped the buckboard and looked close at the young man who sat at his side.

'Always be honest with me,' he said quietly. 'If you ever want to quit, just come and tell me straight out. Play it fair with me and I'll play it fair with you. Have we a deal?'

'We sure have, boss.'

They shook hands and the rig started up again.

'I own a saloon called the Golden Nugget,' Jesse Clark went on. 'I also control the gambling in the other saloon and in one of the hotels. I lend money to folk who can't raise a loan from the bank. That adds to my sins. I get called a Shylock. It don't seem to apply to Banker Ryan. He's a moneylending fella who gets respect. I also got me a gun store and a few other financial interests around the territory. Just to play it safe, I've got the marshal on my payroll. He knows which side he's on if trouble starts. That's the set-up, Sam. Does it scare you?'

The youth grinned. 'Not really, boss. I've been scared all my life.'

'I reckon so. You and me will get along fine.'

His words were almost a temptation to Providence because it was at that moment that a shot exploded somewhere behind them and the bullet passed close enough to the horse for it to rear in fright.

THREE

Jesse Clark cursed vidily as he fought to get control of the animal. When it again answered to the reins, he took the opportunity to look behind him. There was no sign of a pursuer against the darkened sky and he glanced to right and left to scan the various clumps of windswept bushes that littered the sides of the trail.

'Where in hell did that shot come from, Sam?' he asked a little nervously.

'I reckon it came from those trees up on the rise,' the black man replied as he licked his lips. 'Maybe some friends of them hangin' fellas is after us.'

Jesse stopped the rig and reached under the seat for the Winchester. He checked that there was a cartridge in the breech and stood up to get a better view.

'It ain't them, Sam,' he said quietly. 'I figure as how the only one I left alive was heading due east to the Thomas place. This has to be some other bushwhacker. See anything?'

'No, boss, but I can hear horses. Just beyond that rise.'

'You got good hearing, lad. Take the reins and I'll see if we can give them a nasty surprise.'

He waited patiently as two riders appeared

over a ridge. They were dim silhouettes against the sky and came to a halt when they sighted the buckboard.

'Well, they didn't do the shooting,' Jesse mused. 'Must be some other fella around.'

Two more riders appeared as he spoke. They had been hidden by a drift of windswept trees and one of them waved a carbine as he urged his horse towards the rig.

Jesse Clark raised the Winchester to his shoulder and stood like a large statue as the horsemen drew near. He pulled the trigger and one of the animals went down on its side, throwing the rider into a heap of cactus. The man jumped to his feet and ran for cover while his horse kicked aimlessly around.

'You missed him, boss,' Sam said in a neutral voice.

'I didn't aim for him, lad. A man's a small target at this range and in this sort of light. So I shot the horse. A man on foot ain't worth a damn out here.'

He raised the rifle again and fired at one of the other horses. It shied and the rider had to hold on tightly to keep control. All three remaining attackers veered away and disappeared below the horizon.

'We scared 'em off for now,' Jesse said quietly. 'So let's get to town before they try again. Keep going on this trail while I watch out for more trouble.'

The black man slapped the reins against the flank of the horse and the rig moved off at a steady pace.

'I'll send out the marshal in the morning to see if there's a brand on that horse. I like to know who's causing trouble on my patch. Are you sorry you took up with me now, Sam?'

The young man grinned in the darkness. 'I reckon as how you can do enough shootin' for both of us, boss. But I sure will be glad to see Santa Rosa.'

'Once we get beyond that next ridge, you'll see the lights. It's a nice little town. A man can have a good life there.'

They topped the ridge ten minutes later and the lights of Santa Rosa threw patterns over the blackness of the night. Figures could be seen moving on the main street and there were occasional flashes of brightness when somebody opened a door or lit another lamp. Jesse Clark breathed a sigh of relief. He did not like excitement and would be glad to see the comfort of his own home.

'There's somebody comin' from town,' Sam said with anxious suddenness. 'Headin' right for us, boss.'

Jesse stood up on the moving rig, cocking the Winchester and pressing the backs of his knees against the seat to keep his balance. He peered into the darkness ahead but it took him a few minutes before he could make out the figure on the horse that was approaching from the town.

He could see the raised right hand and thought for a second that a gun was being aimed. Then he realized that the man was waving frantically to attract the attention of the two on the buckboard.

'Pull up, Sam,' Jesse said as he sat down again. 'I reckon to know who it is and we got no need to fret.'

The rig stopped and the two men watched the approaching horseman as he galloped up the slope to meet them. It was fully dark now with the stars brilliant in a velvet sky. Jesse had to peer hard to recognize the features of his right-hand man.

It was Pete Willet, a fiftyish, wizened little fellow who looked after Jesse's interests with long-term devotion while he carved off the odd dollar here and there that he thought his boss did not know about. Jesse knew, but Pete was loyal, and that was what counted. Jesse did not expect any of his people to be any more honest than he was.

The man pulled up his small roan mare by the side of the rig and glanced curiously at the young man who sat holding the reins. Jesse Clark introduced them and the newcomer nodded a little suspiciously to the new employee.

'I take it that this ain't a welcoming-home

ceremony, Pete,' Jesse said tautly. 'You was waiting for me down there like some guardian angel. How long have you been watching out for my arrival?'

'I'm not sure, boss, but I reckon two hours or more. Ever since the Morland boys and Bill Grover left town.'

Jesse looked across at young Sam. 'They must have been the four we just ran into. They seem to have taken fright and made themselves scarce now.'

'Well they was talkin' real big in town earlier on, boss. Sayin' as how they was goin' to lynch you or blow you to hell and back.'

Jesse Clark sucked his teeth. 'And why should the Morland boys be out to make trouble for me?' he asked. 'I ain't done them no harm.'

'Old Ma Pendry was in Santa Rosa. And she's their aunt.'

'Oh.' Jesse fell silent for a little while. That was something he had not reckoned with.

'And I suppose they got kinda riled when she told them about selling the ranch to me?' he asked.

'You got the right of it there, boss. When she told them what you paid for it, they went on the rampage and ended up by goin' into the Golden Nugget, and tellin' folk that your games was crooked. They started bad-mouthin' you all over town and then smashed up the saloon real bad.'

'And what the hell was Marshal Hogan doing while all this was going on?'

Pete shrugged. 'Well, at first, he seemed all for throwin' them in jail, but the mayor came on the scene and held him back. Told him to check on the gamin' tables and the decks of cards. He called the marshal off and the town started gettin' real mad. You can't go back there, boss. You have to get away till this settles down again. I'm scared to hell myself, but when them fellas left town, I figured as how I'd better warn you.'

Jesse stirred uneasily on the sprung seat. 'Yeah, I can see how the mayor would be pleased for me to be in trouble. He's not been a friend since that little deal with the timber went sour. They all knew I'd be coming back today, and that banker fella had a meeting set with me in the morning. Is he in it as well?'

Pete nodded glumly.

'So they've all forgotten who lines their pockets. I suppose him and the mayor were yapping around like a couple of prairie dogs?'

'As soon as the Morland brothers started things moving,' Pete said. 'The mayor wanted to be popular, and with him and the marshal doin' nothing, it was an open town, boss.'

'And what about my house?' Jesse asked in a tight voice. 'Is that safe?'

'A few kids threw stones at the windows and your fencin' has been knocked down. But nobody's done any real damage yet. The gun store was broke open and I reckon that all your best stock has been took. Limey Baker tried to stop 'em but he just got a hidin' and his wife packed him off home. You can't go back there, boss.'

Jesse fidgeted uneasily. He kept glancing around in the darkness as if expecting another attack. The other two men waited silently as he made up his mind.

'I wonder how brave they'll be if I just ride into town and face 'em,' he said after a while. 'Most of their courage probably came from drinking my liquor. They might not feel as brave when they see me.'

Pete Willet grimaced in the darkness. 'I ain't told you the worst, boss,' he muttered. 'The mayor has ordered Marshal Hogan to arrest you on sight. Them gamblin'-tables really upset folks. As soon as you put a foot in town, I reckon they'll have you locked away in the jailhouse.'

'I see. So they've got me all sewn up. Well, I suppose I'd better head south across the border. You know where I'll be staying, Pete, so you can send me a message if things change. And I reckon they soon will. That town needs my money, and given a little time for tempers to cool down, I figure they'll be asking me back home again.'

He patted Pete Willet on his bony shoulder.

'Thanks for the warning, Pete,' he said in a voice that was back to its normal calm. 'Here's twenty dollars to keep you going, and I'll send a letter to that damned bank authorizing you to draw expenses. You can tell Limey to re-open the gun store when it's safe, and you oversee the repairs to the saloon. Get new decks of cards and break up the tables they're complaining about. That should pacify them. We need to get things back to normal as soon as possible. This will pass quickly enough when tempers cool and the marshal wakes up to the fact that his pay-packet won't be as big as it used to be.'

Pete grinned. 'I'm not to take his usual ten dollars to the jailhouse?' he asked.

'Not till he remembers who runs Santa Rosa.'

Jesse Clark turned to the man who shared the buckboard seat with him.

'Well, Sam, things haven't worked out as we'd hoped. If you want to get down now and head for Santa Rosa with Pete, you're under no obligation. He'll show you where you can get shelter and a meal, and he might even be able to find you a job.'

The young man grinned in the darkness.

'If it's all right with you, boss,' he said cheerfully, 'I'll drive this rig across the border for you.'

Jesse nodded. 'That's fine with me, fella. I could certainly use some company right now.'

FOUR

The black gelding tapped the shallow water with its foreleg as it drank. The noise of the iron-shod hoof echoed from the steep grassy slopes that ran north and south under the hot afternoon sun. Nogales trading post had been left behind and Bill Hardman was now on foreign soil.

He had ridden from Tucson, past the old mission of Tumacacori, across the Rio Altar, and into the deserted valleys and mountains of northern Mexico. He sweated as his horse drank. There were still some miles to go, and only the advance in pay that he had been given, and the promise of more, was urging him on.

Bill Hardman had once been a lawman, but a shoot-out with a crooked marshal had cost him the job and nobody in authority would employ him in Arizona or Texas. He had become a hired gun. But with one difference. He was a hired gun who could be trusted. His reputation for honest dealing had helped him to earn a living when no official body would give him a job.

And now he had been called to Mexico with a promise of bigger money than he had ever been offered. All he possessed was in the saddle-bags, and his tall, lean frame with darkly tanned face, sat the gentle gelding with easy competence. He was not a good-looking young man, but the eyes under the broad Stetson were clear and sharp, and the mouth a firm line.

He was now heading in the direction of the Sierra Madre range, having avoided numerous army patrols and keeping clear of the few small towns and villages on his route. After a spectacular hold-up and murder a few weeks earlier, the United States cavalry were out in force along the border, and Bill Hardman was not anxious to be seen by them.

The Mexican army also seemed to have more patrols out than usual, their horses moving in small troops from village to village. The two military forces appeared to be working together and the young rider had felt it wiser to travel at night, where possible over rough ground at the base of the mountains that loomed on every side.

His goal was a small ranch that lay in a valley among the foothills of a wooded mass of snow-capped peaks. The man he was looking for was from Arizona, but someone who found it safer to be buried away in the wilds of Mexico.

Jesse Clark had sent him a letter that had taken three weeks to reach Tucson. It was a generous offer of work, based on Bill's own reputation for straight dealing. He had heard of Jesse as a big businessman from a little town near the border where one or two people could dominate a whole community if they had wealth. The man now seemed to be in some sort of trouble and had not only sent fifty dollars in a bank draft, but had provided a map of how to reach the tucked-away ranch in a foreign country.

Bill spurred his horse out of the little stream and set off again heading due south before turning slightly west between lower hills where a keen wind cooled the air as he camped for the night.

His journey was completed early the next morning. He had to travel in daylight now. The ground was unfamiliar and he was getting near his goal.

When he saw the place it was clear that it was not really a ranch, but more like a small farm with a few milking-cows in the pasture, some hogs running wild, and a profusion of poultry that pecked at everything in sight. Bill smiled to himself. To imagine the towns-man Jesse Clark as a farmer was not some-thing to be easily accepted. He saw the house in the distance. It was an off-white adobe building, quite small, and with a chimney at one end which was throwing off some smoke. Somebody was probably making breakfast. The house was surrounded by a low adobe wall with a wide entrance-gate, while the fields all around were either pasture or sown with maize. Behind the adobe structure was a wooden barn and some other low buildings that looked like stables.

The place was quiet and only cattle paid attention as he neared it. Bill Hardman was taken by surprise when a door suddenly opened as he entered the little courtyard. A man came out of the house with a shotgun in his arms. He was a black fellow, young and well built. His face bore a slightly uneasy expression as he pointed the weapon at the visitor.

'What you want here, mister?' the young man barked.

'I'm Bill Hardman and Mr Clark's expectin' me,' the horseman answered calmly. 'You can put the gun away and tell him I'm here.'

'Welcome to my humble abode.'

It was not the young man who spoke but a large, fat fellow who filled the doorway of the little house and beamed at the visitor. Jesse Clark was dressed informally in a grey flannel shirt and canvas trousers. He wore an old straw hat on the back of his head and carried a cigar in his podgy left hand. He was in a good mood as he ushered Bill Hardman into the building.

It was a neat place, furnished with locally made pieces and with a cooking-hearth near which the coffee-pot bubbled and a skillet spurted fat as it cooked some large rashers of ham.

'You're just in time for a meal,' the fat man said cheerfully. 'It's a long journey from

Tucson and you'll be glad of a roof over your head at last. I'd near given up on you.'

'It took the best part of three weeks for your letter to get to me, Mr Clark.'

'Ah, the postal service. It never changes.' The fat man looked round the little room. 'Not exactly a palace, is it, Mr Hardman?'

He waved Bill to a chair and the two men accepted the large mugs of coffee that Sam placed in front of them.

'I've had to leave my own place in Santa Rosa and take a temporary refuge here,' Jesse Clark went on. 'Things at home have gone amiss and I've lost everything for the time being. Businesses, house, people I thought were my friends. Everything. And that includes something of particular value, my dear boy. That's why I've sent for you.'

Bill Hardman took a sip of the scalding coffee. It was the best he had tasted since starting out from Tucson.

'I'll do what I can,' he said a little cautiously.

'I know you will. Now then, I hope you

were discreet in your travelling?'

'You mean, keepin' out of sight of the patrols? Are they worryin' you, Mr Clark?'

Jesse looked surprised at the question.

'No, not them,' he said dismissively. 'I'm worried about some of the folk from Santa Rosa who've already tried to kill me. This is my sister's place and I've sent her and her family into town so that they'll be safe if anyone does hunt me down. There are just two day labourers working the fields for the time being. This fella here, by the way, is Sam. Do you know what a major-domo is, Mr Hardman?'

The young man shook his head and looked quizzically at the grinning Sam.

'Well, he's a sort of odd-job fella who can be trusted,' Jesse explained. 'And there ain't many folks I'd say that about in these times. Now then, Bill, you'd best rest up for a day or so before you start back across the border. You've got plenty more journeying ahead of you.'

'What exactly is my job, Mr Clark?' Bill

asked as he spread his hands towards the warmth of the hearth.

'Well, I'll tell you, son.'

Jesse moved to a large rocking-chair that creaked dangerously beneath his weight.

'I was living high on the hog in Santa Rosa when they ran me out of town. I've had a message from somebody there I can still rely on, and he tells me that my businesses are being run by other folk, that the marshal wants me arrested, and that my home has been emptied by the folks who once kissed my ass if I as much as frowned on them.'

He paused to light another cigar with a wooden spill. 'There's a little package hidden away,' he said, 'and I want you to get it for me. It contains what's left of my ready cash and I don't aim to leave it lying about in Santa Rosa doing nothing that'll profit me.'

Bill looked hard at the benign face of the man who sat opposite him.

'You did say that you had one man in Santa Rosa you could still rely on,' he said quietly. 'Why don't he collect the money for you?'

He was greeted by a gale of belly-shaking laughter.

'Oh, Mr Hardman, you are an innocent in this cruel world!' the fat man chortled. 'Pete Willet is as loyal to me as Sam here. But he steals, Mr Hardman. He steals. Just a few dollars here and there, but I'll wager that he more than doubles what I pay him. A man can be loyal, my dear sir, and still be tempted by a large sum of money. I would not wish to put him in that sad position. He might succumb.'

'I see. So what exactly do I do?'

'Well now, there is an Imperial stove in the front bedroom of my house. It is set on stone slabs and the stovepipe runs up the wall and out the side of the building. Now, it's too old a stove for folk to steal, and nobody is going to play around with worn slabs that are covered in ash. One of those slabs lifts, and under it is a small package the size of one of those romantic novellas that so amuse the dear ladies. That is your goal. It's wrapped in oiled silk, sealed with wax, and tied around with string. That was done as a precaution against spilled water. Get that package and bring it to me. That's your job.'

'It seems a little too easy the way you say it, Mr Clark,' Bill said thoughtfully. 'Have you told me everything?'

The fat man laughed again, displaying his perfect teeth.

'A shrewd question, young sir,' he acknowledged cheerfully. 'Pete Willet has had to leave town, and anybody who goes near my house is certain to be an object of curiosity. They all want to know where I keep my cash money, and some of them still have a liking for a lynching party as an added-bonus. You'll have to be mighty careful.'

He tossed the remains of the chewed cigar into the hearth.

'There's another problem,' he said in a more serious voice. 'I had a certain lady – you know what I mean – and I am told that she has moved her affections elsewhere. She'll also be watching, and she occupies the house next door. Don't trust her, young fellow. She's in love with money.'

'And I get five hundred dollars for this little chore, Mr Clark?' Bill asked.

'Less the fifty I sent you with the letter. And all paid on the delivery of that packet. Agreed?'

He held out a chubby hand on which sat a large gold signet ring. Bill took it and they shook on the deal.

'Agreed,' he said.

'There is just one more thing, Bill,' Jesse Clark said quietly. 'I want you to bring Pete Willet back here.'

'Why?'

'Pete's last message said that he had to move to a little cabin that we use way out in the mountains. The Santa Rosa folks don't like anybody who might be loyal to me. I'll tell you how to reach him, and after you've picked up the money, you can go meet him and get the little fella safely across the border. I owe him that.'

'I'll do that, Mr Clark.'

'Good. And one other thing. Pete will be very useful in getting you safe here. He knows the border like the back of his hand. We've carried on a few business deals that would have been spoiled by nosy army patrols. So you can rely on him to steer you through the present shindig. I wouldn't want you searched by the blue-bellies while you were carrying my poke. Pete will also be able to show you a good way of hiding it.'

Bill nodded his agreement and the discussion became more general about life in Tucson, while Sam cooked more food and the room warmed up.

Bill Hardman set off the next morning. He carried fresh supplies, full water bottles, and his horse was lively after a good night's rest with plenty to eat and drink. Jesse Clark and Sam waved him off as he left the little farm and headed north again.

He travelled with a feeling almost of relief that he had work to do and was ready for whatever lay ahead. The weather was dry and getting hotter, with a slight breeze coming off the surrounding mountains to cool the air a little and make riding a pleasant experience.

He stopped for the night by a small creek that was clear and fast as the water came down from the mountains to rattle noisily over a stony bed of gravel. It was cold, fresh from the snowline and the steady sound of it was like a comforting lullaby as he lay down to sleep and pulled the blanket over his shoulders.

It was his horse that gave the alarm. It woke him from a confused dream by suddenly letting out a whinny as something disturbed its rest.

Bill Hardman reached under the blanket for his gun and was already rising on one elbow when he felt the barrel of another weapon placed against the side of his head.

FIVE

The steel was cold and held steadily as a voice spoke softly in the cool darkness.

'You make one wrong move, fella, and I reckon on you as bein' a dead man.'

Bill Hardman nodded his head slowly. His long experience kept him calm and calculating.

'I ain't movin' none,' he said quietly. 'You've got the drop on me. There's a few dollars in my poke if it's money you're after.'

'I'm not after your money, fella. I want to know who in hell you are?'

Bill twisted a little to try and make out the features of the other man in the darkness. His hand still gripped the pistol beneath the blanket and he had it levelled at his opponent.

'My name's Hardman,' he said humbly,

'and I'm on my way to Santa Rosa.'

'Bill Hardman?' There was a note of surprise in the other man's voice.

'That's right. Do you know me?'

'I surely do,' the man replied with a laugh.

Bill felt the cold steel removed from the side of his head and heard the click as the man uncocked the gun. The fellow stood up and crossed to the dying fire. He kicked it alight and put on some brushwood to flare up and lighten the darkness. Bill could see him now, silhouetted against the sky. He was a tall man, heavily built, who seemed familiar even before the light fell on his features.

'Well, if it isn't Bert Ebdon!' he exclaimed as he dropped his own gun under the blanket and rose to his feet. The two men shook hands and Bill added some water to the coffee-pot before putting it over the fire.

Bert Ebdon had been a handsome man in his day, but he was now in his fifties, grey, lined, and with a bitter mouth that was grim and turned down at the corners. He was a man who looked as if life had used him savagely and who did not expect things to get better.

The two were sitting side by side a few minutes later with tin mugs of hot coffee in their hands.

'I think you've got some explainin' to do,' Bill Hardman suggested. 'Wakin' up with a gun in the head is not what I expect from an old friend.'

The other man laughed. 'Well, I'll tell you, fella. I've been trailin' you since you left Jesse Clark's place, but keepin' my distance while I did it. I had no idea it could be young Bill Hardman. So I figured on enquirin' all peaceful-like. You workin' for Jesse?'

'And if I am?'

'Well, we might just get to cross-purposes. I suppose you've heard about the reputation that fella's gotten himself?'

Bill nodded. 'I've heard tell that he weren't no angel, but he don't try hidin' it from folks. What quarrel have you got with him?'

'None, but I'm bein' paid to keep an eye

on the fella. And on anybody he has dealings with. I'm a Pinkerton agent these days.'

Bill Hardman was silent for a moment. The words had been spoken with a certain pride and he realized the need for caution.

'Well, that *is* news,' he said slowly. 'Should I be offerin' congratulations?'

Bill Ebdon shrugged in the darkness. 'I don't rightly know, but at least it beats workin' as a deputy in some two-bit town. The money's a little better and the risks are less. I'll tell you how it is, Bill. There's been a big dust-up back across the border. A colonel's wife was killed and robbed. The whole area's bein' patrolled on both sides and there's a big reward for the killers.'

'I heard about it. Two women were killed,' Bill said quietly as he gave himself time to think.

The other man shook his head dismissively. 'The other was only a servin' maid she had with her. It's the colonel's wife the army's concerned about. They're mighty riled up about it. Two of their own men was killed as well, and none of that sits sweetly with them military fellas.'

'So who called in the Pinkerton people?'

'Ah, well, that's where it gets a bit mixed up, Bill. The official line is that Mrs Barstin's jewellery was what the hold-up fellas was after. I reckon that it was worth all of two hundred dollars. But she was carryin' somethin' else, and that's givin' certain folks the real fidgets.'

'Now you're gettin' interesting, Bert.'

'There was a package, so I'm told, and it's reckoned to be as valuable as hell. The hold-up men killed her for that, but nobody ain't puttin' that out to the newspapers. Pinkerton's have been employed by someone who's real involved and who's put up another reward that's one of the biggest I've ever seen on offer.'

'Could it be political?'

Bert shrugged. 'I know nothin' about it, Bill, but it sure sounds like it. I could retire on a reward like that.'

'So what's it got to do with Jesse Clark?'

Bert Ebdon snorted. 'You might well ask. Clark is a mighty busy fella around Santa Rosa. He left town a couple of months back, met someone just outside Tucson, and then headed for home again. While he was away, the local folks found out too much about his crooked dealin' and made it clear they didn't want him back in town. So he headed for Mexico. I think he knows somethin' about that package, and if he does, you could be involved.'

'How?'

Bert Ebdon threw the dregs of his coffee on to the ground. His eyes were hard as he looked at his companion.

'You didn't make no social call back there, fella. It could be that you just delivered that package to him. Or maybe you've been hired to pick it up from somewhere. Whichever way it goes, that could be a mighty bad thing. Folks was killed for it.'

There was a short silence between the two men and only the crackling of the fire and the movement of the horses disturbed the night air. Sparks flew up into the sky to be wafted away by the wind as Bill Hardman thought about his position. He finally made a decision.

'You may have somethin' there, Bert,' he said quietly. 'Have you got one of them papers about you that the Pinkerton people use to identify their agents?'

The older man nodded and reached into his waistcoat pocket to extract a shabby envelope, which he passed across. Bill opened it and read the creased sheet of paper which bore the letter-heading of the detective agency. It authorized Bert Ebdon to represent them. As a former marshal, Bill had seen such documents several times and was able to accept it without question. He handed back the envelope.

'I got a letter from Jesse Clark,' he explained. 'He wants me to go to Santa Rosa, get into his house, and pick up a parcel of money that he has hidden there. His bank account is safe enough and he seems to have plenty of ready cash on him, but this money comes to a few thousand dollars and he don't want it left where folks might be makin' free with his belongings.'

'I see. Then I got no quarrel with you, Bill. But do me and yo'self one service. Open that package and make sure that it really is only money.'

'I'll do that. I wouldn't want to be used by a fella who was mixed up in the killin' of women. Are you sure you don't know what's in this package you was talkin' about?'

Bert Ebdon grinned sourly. 'I could make guesses,' he said, 'but I'm not bein' paid to do that. It might be safer not to know. One thing is for sure. It ain't money and it don't belong to Jesse Clark.'

'You got yourself a deal then,' Bill Hardman said. 'I'll make certain sure that it's his moneypoke and nothin' else. Now I reckon we should get some sleep. I got a long ride ahead of me. What do you reckon to do?'

Bert Ebdon got up to go and unsaddle his horse.

'Well, I figure on watchin' Jesse Clark's

hide-out for a while longer. He might have some other visitors. Y'see, Bill, he was meetin' with real suspicious folk in Tucson and makin' some sort of deal. Every law-enforcement agency along the border is on the lookout and we're passin' information along. There's also that reward, and I could sure use that, or even a part of it.'

'Is the reward for the package or for the killers?'

Bert Ebdon grinned. 'Officially, it's for the killers. But there ain't much doubt that it's the packet they're after.'

The two men went to sleep shortly afterwards and the fire died down.

Bill Hardman reached Santa Rosa three days later. It was a small town with three saloons, a decent hotel, a few stores, and a large school house next to a wooden church. The place was built mostly in the Mexican style of small adobe buildings with streaked white frontages. The commercial premises were more Anglo in their style, new redbrick or timbered structures bleached by a strong sun.

Bill had a plan of the town, roughly drawn by Jesse Clark. It showed him where the marshal's office lay and where Jesse's wooden house stood in a back lane with a kitchen-garden and corral to the rear. He skirted round the edge of the town, keeping the broad hat low over his eyes. It was getting dark as he rode along the rutted lane where the house he wanted stood over to his right.

There were similar houses on either side of it, each in its little plot of land. The one nearest to him was a picture of trim fencing and neat hedges. He smiled slightly. It was a very feminine statement and appeared out of place in such a rough-looking town.

Jesse Clark's house was quite large. Its woodwork was creosoted and the windows were outlined in white paint. There was a beaten-earth path to the front porch and a rocking-chair sat there as though waiting for the owner to occupy it.

The windows were smashed. Glass littered

the path and the wooden stoop. The front door was ajar and the panel nearest the lock was split at a point where somebody's boot had smashed it open.

Bill rode past as though having no interest in the place. The buildings opposite the houses were the backs of stores and there were no lights showing. The neat-looking house had a light in the front room and except for that the lane was dark and getting darker as night fell.

He rode back to the main street and tethered his mount outside a saloon called the Golden Nugget. It was a cheerful and noisy place with a dozen other horses waiting patiently outside while their owners enjoyed a drink and a chance at the faro-tables.

Bill noticed that a sign in one of the windows told the world that the premises were under new management. He climbed the steps, and entered the smoky room where nobody paid any attention to another customer. The beer was good and he looked around with interest at what had once belonged to Jesse Clark. He drank the beer slowly, waiting for the night to get darker; waiting for respectable folk to be going to bed, and when a prowling man in a back lane might not be noticed.

The moon was absorbed by clouds when he left the saloon two hours later. He walked down the street and turned into the back lane where Jesse Clark's house lay neglected and forlorn. He was no longer wearing spurs and his horse was still outside the saloon, happy in the company of other animals that would still have an hour or so to wait for their drinking and gambling owners.

After the noise on the main street the back lanes were quiet save for the scuttling of an occasional rat. The neat house next to Jesse's was now in darkness as Bill Hardman moved slowly between the two buildings until he reached the back door of the one he was seeking. He had a key in his hand, supplied by the owner, and it fitted snugly into the lock and turned quietly.

The kitchen smelled damp and cold as he entered and closed the door behind him. There was glass on the floor from broken window panes and two cupboards had been ransacked of food and crockery. His toe hit a damaged cup that rolled a few inches before lying still again. There was another door ahead of him, partly open and leading to a hallway with a room on either side. He could see the front door, still ajar and throwing some vague light into the building.

There was no furniture. The walls had been stripped of clocks and paintings. Only a carpet lay on the floor, too badly damaged for anybody to bother stealing it. He moved down the hallway until encountering the staircase. The treads creaked as he moved slowly upwards, feeling his way carefully along the wall.

Jesse Clark had told him that his bedroom was at the front of the building. The door to it was open and scarred where someone had been dragging furniture out on to the landing. There was a smell of charred wood in the air, and as the moon broke through the low cloud for a moment, Bill could see the remains of a small fire in one corner of the room. It had just been a spilled oil-lamp, the remains of which still lay amid the mess of smoke-streaked walls and blackened ceiling.

The stove he was looking for was on the wall to his left. It was a well-polished affair, pot-bellied and large, like its owner. The black-leaded chimney climbed the wall and exited through to the open air.

He could see the stone slabs on which it stood. Ashes had fallen down and lay in a thick mat on the surface. The only disturbance were the pawmarks of a mouse hunting for food.

Bill Hardman felt in his waistcoat pocket for the little copper Vesta box that he carried. There was also the stub of a tallow candle, and he knelt down in front of the stove to give some light to the scene of his work.

At that moment he heard the creaking of

the stairs. It was very faint. Fainter than it had been when he climbed them, but it was quite distinct and he reached for his gun as he waited in the darkness.

The moon vanished again behind the clouds and he could see nothing through the open doorway. It was silent now and his nerves were tense as he pointed the .44 at whoever must enter.

The crash of glass took him by surprise. The window behind him had suddenly shattered with a loud screech of flying shards. It had already been broken and letting in the cool night air, but now another pane splintered and he turned towards the noise with the gun cocked and ready for use.

It was the wrong move and he knew it instantly. Two shots came from the doorway with flashes that lit up the room.

SIX

Bill Hardman ducked as he swung back towards the door. He heard the bullets hitting the wall behind him as he dived for the floor and rolled over.

He raised the Colt to fire through the opening and was just going to pull the trigger at the vague figure he could see on the landing, when he realized that it was a woman.

He made an awkward dive through the doorway and threw his arms around the shadowy form. She screamed and struggled as the pistol dropped from her hand and clattered on the bare boards. He pinned her to the wall as her fists battered him and her strong legs kicked out wildly.

'Cut it out, lady!' he shouted. 'I ain't goin' to harm you, but I don't like folks shootin' at me.'

'Let go of me, you no-good Yankee! This is my house you're stealin' from.'

'Is that a fact? Well, it bein' empty an' all, I figured it would make a good spot for a night's rest. The front door was open and one hell of a lot more invitin' than you are. And there ain't really a thing worth stealin' round here, lady.'

'Well, it ain't a hotel for tramps, so get the hell out!' she shouted.

'Now, look, lady, suppose we do a deal. You stop kickin' and hollerin', and I'll stop holdin' you tight. How about it?'

'I want my gun back.'

'Only when I'm sure you ain't figurin' to shoot me. That was one neat trick, throwin' somethin' through the window. I could have got real hurt if you'd been a better shot.'

Her body stiffened angrily in his grasp.

'I'm a perfectly good shot!' she cried. 'But it's as dark as hell in here.'

'Let's have some light then,' Bill suggested.

He let go of her and stepped back a few paces. His left foot hit the pistol she had dropped and he picked it up. It was an old-fashioned Navy Colt and he tucked it into his belt as he went back into the room to strike a Vesta.

The candle-stub threw a warm glow over the scene as he placed it on the old stove, where it flickered in the draught from the shattered windows.

He could see the woman now. She was young and well-bodied. Her hair was dark, long in the Mexican style and held by a comb at each side of her head. Her lips were full, almost pouting, and her eyes shone angrily in the candlelight. She watched him for a moment before taking a few more steps to enter the room.

'Who are you?' she asked. Her voice was calmer now as though she sensed that he meant her no harm.

'I'm a stray, lady,' Bill said cheerfully. 'Just lookin' for somewhere to spend the night and not havin' money for a hotel bill. This place was empty so I decided to use it.'

She came closer. Her eyes were on the gun

that he had picked up from the floor.

'Don't try goin' for it, ma'am,' he warned her. 'I don't aim for you to start shootin' again.'

She gave a tight smile. 'You were lucky,' she said.

'Yes. Lucky you missed.'

'I didn't aim to hit you.'

Bill patted the gun. 'A young lady like you shouldn't be playin' around with these things. Especially an old piece like this. They just ain't reliable.'

'That was my pappy's, fella, and I can outshoot a lot of men with their new fancy Colts. You got a name?'

'Sure. What about you?'

'I'm Helen McCourt and my house is next door. Now, suppose you tell me your name.'

'Why not? I'm Bill Hardman, lookin' for work and pretty anxious to get some sleep.'

'So you just picked this place? How did you get in?'

'The front door is open, ma'am, and I could see that it's empty and knocked about a little. Seemed the right place to settle.'

She came closer as if her courage was returning. Bill was wary. Her rustling grey skirt brushed the dusty floor and her tight bodice did nothing to hide her figure. He knew who she was now and was aware of the danger in this young woman.

'You're one hell of a liar, fella,' she said bluntly. 'You came in by the back door, and you used a key. Did Jesse send you?'

'Jesse?'

'Jesse Clark. He gave you his key and sent you to collect the money. Don't try tellin' me no different. Have you found it?'

Bill shook his head sadly. 'You lost me somewhere back there, ma am,' he said in a puzzled voice. 'I'm just a saddle tramp.'

'Like hell you are. Now understand me clearly, fella. There's a parcel of money somewhere in this house. The place has been torn apart by the locals but I don't reckon as any of them found it. Jesse always had ready cash around but he hid it well. I was his woman and I figure that if he can't have it, I'm next in line.'

Bill Hardman took the old Navy Colt from his belt and pulled the percussion caps off the nipples. He dropped them on to the floor and handed the pistol back to Helen McCourt. She took it silently and watched as he walked past her to the landing. He was half-way down the stairs before she spoke.

'Where are you going to, fella?' she shouted.

He turned to face her as she leaned over the rail.

'To find somewhere else to stay for the night. I ain't welcome here and I don't aim to get mixed up in no family feud.'

His footsteps echoed through the empty building as he walked out of the front door and back to the saloon to collect his horse. He rode out of town in a thoughtful mood. It puzzled him that the smashing of the window and the two shots had not attracted any attention. Nobody seemed interested, and that was odd, and dangerous. It could mean that anything to do with Jesse Clark and Helen McCourt was strictly private.

He slept that night by a small creek that seemed to draw all the creatures of the darkness to drink and scuttle around there. The air got chill and a wind came up that only fell as the sun rose mistily over the distant mountains.

Bill Hardman looked at the little map that Jesse Clark had drawn for him. It showed a small canyon where Pete Willet would be hiding out in the tiny cabin that he had there. It was about fifteen miles away from where Bill was camped, but he reckoned that now was the time that he needed the only other man Jesse Clark trusted.

He set off at a steady pace towards the eastern mountains, resting his horse every few miles and taking a long break in the afternoon until the heat of the day had passed.

The canyon was a low, narrow place with reddish walls and stunted plants that showed the scarcity of water. The walls were too sloping for the hoofs of his horse to echo as he rode down the narrow, boulder-strewn trail that ran along the side of a tiny, yellowish stream.

He could see smoke rising round the next bend and, as the hut came in sight, he could hear the distinct click of a hammer going back on a concealed gun.

'Pete Willet!' he shouted. 'Jesse sent me. My name's Bill Hardman and he says I've got to take you down to Mexico with me.'

There was a long silence while Bill looked at the little cabin that snuggled against the wall of the canyon. It was built of roughly hewn sandstone with the joints stuffed by clay and a piece of canvas across the window-space. The roof was of dried turf, above which rose an iron chimney which was smoking furiously.

He thought that he could see a gun barrel poking from under the canvas, but the sun was in his eyes and he could not be sure. He was just going to call again when a voice issued from the cabin.

'If you've seen Jesse lately,' the voice shouted, 'you'll know who he's got with him. Tell me, fella.'

Bill grinned. Pete Willet was nobody's fool.

'He's got a black man called Sam. Tall, young fella. That right?'

There was another short silence and then the door of the cabin opened to disclose a little man who blinked in the light and came forward a few paces. He carried a shotgun but did not seem hostile.

'I guess you're the right fella,' he said as he neared the stranger. Jesse told me in his letter to expect somebody. He said you was honest.'

'That's right.'

The little man managed a tight grin. 'Well, me and Jesse ain't accustomed to havin' honest folk around. I guess I'll just have to get used to it. You'd better tend your horse and then come in and have a meal.'

There were beans, bacon, and strong coffee eventually laid out in the little cabin.

The place had an earth floor and smelled musty, but the aroma of the hot coffee was welcoming and Pete Willet even apologized for not having any bread. The two men sat on either side of the rough table to enjoy their meal.

'Are you in touch with Helen McCourt?' Bill asked after a while. 'Can you get a message to her?'

Pete looked at him uncertainly. 'I don't reckon to that woman,' he said bluntly. 'And I don't think the boss trusts her.'

Bill nodded. 'You're both right there. She tried shootin' me when I visited Jesse's place.'

'Did you get the money?' Pete's voice was eager. 'If you have it, we can get the hell out for Mexico. I'm scared of stayin' around here.'

'No, I didn't get the money. She was watchin' the place like a hungry buzzard. I want to get her away for half an hour or so. And I'll need your help.'

Pete's knife clattered on the tin plate.

'I ain't goin' back to town,' he said fearfully. 'It just ain't healthy.'

'Look, Pete, can you get her a message to meet you somewhere safe?'

Willet thought about it for a moment. 'I reckon so,' he said slowly. 'There's an Indian fella who'll take a message into Santa Rosa for the price of a jar of corn mash. He won't go talkin' to folk and he's as close-mouthed as you could wish. I'd be happy to meet her out of town. She's got a little buggy and we could meet up somewhere round Parvo Creek. I could watch her comin' from there and make sure she had no company. What message would I be givin' her though?'

Bill thought about it for a moment and then grinned as a thought struck him.

'Tell her that Jesse sent you a message that a fella called Bill Hardman is headin' for Santa Rosa and she's to give him all the help she can.'

'That's one hell of a message for a gal who's been tryin' to shoot you,' the little man chortled.

'Yes, but it will get her out of town for a while, and make her think that you and me has never met up. Arrange the meetin' for late at night and I'll be in and outa that house in a couple of shakes.'

Pete Willet's greedy little eyes shone in the dimness of the cabin.

'You know exactly where the money is, then?' he asked.

Bill nodded.

'And I suppose you know why the boss wouldn't let me collect it for him?'

Bill nodded again and grinned. The little man grinned back.

'I couldn't stay honest at the sight of all them dollars,' he admitted. 'So he got you in. An honest man.'

He laughed at the joke but there was an edge to his hilarity.

They finished the meal and Bill Hardman spent the night in the little cabin. Pete Willet set off to meet his Indian friend the next morning while the other man planned his campaign.

Nobody in Santa Rosa really knew what he looked like, and even Helen McCourt had only seen him by the light of a candle. If he went back and waited until she left town in her buggy, he could slip into the empty house, dig up the packet, and be away before anybody knew what was happening.

It was still light when he got into town. The main street was reasonably busy and a few stores were open to get the last of the trade. Bill Hardman wore his trail coat this time and had changed his shirt for one of a darker colour. He had also omitted to shave since his last visit, and it did not seem likely that anyone would pay attention to him.

He knew by speaking to Pete Willet that Helen McCourt would have to come out of the back lane and pass along the main street to reach Parvo Creek and meet the little man. He was just hoping that his judgement was sound. He stood outside the Golden Nugget for a few minutes, loosening the girth of his horse and weighing up the activity on the street.

The marshal's office was closed and, although the dusk was now falling, there was no light in the building. The saloon behind him was nearly empty and a young lad in the gun store that had once belonged to Jesse Clark was putting up the wooden shutters.

He went into the saloon, bought a beer, and stood by the window as he slowly drank it. The place was warm and the absence of noise was oddly disturbing. The only rig that passed on the street was a large cart full of timber, drawn by two heavy horses. He bought another drink and took up his position again.

Then she appeared. Bill had been just about to give up hope for his plan when a small, two-wheeled buggy came past the Golden Nugget at a spanking pace. Helen McCourt was at the reins. Her hair was hidden by a broad hat, tied under the chin. She wore a trail coat similar to the one the watcher was wearing, and her capable hands were gloved as she guided the animal towards the north end of town.

Bill drew a sigh of relief and finished the beer with as much composure as he could muster. With a nod to the bartender, he left the saloon and walked casually down the street to turn into the narrow lane that led to Jesse's house. It was practically dark now and there was nobody about. The front door was still open and someone had stolen the wooden gate and the rocking-chair since his last visit.

He decided to go through the back door as he had done last time. His feet were silent as he moved round the side of the building while taking the key from his pocket ready for use. The lock turned easily and he entered the house with his pulse racing.

Then he smelt it. Somebody was smoking a cigar.

Bill Hardman reached for his gun as he halted to listen for any movement around him. He stood motionless for several minutes with the patience born of long experience as a lawman. The sudden creak of a floorboard came from the room on his right. The door was closed and the place in darkness.

He inwardly cursed the young woman who had left somebody on guard while she was away. He withdrew as silently as he had entered, not attempting to close the back door in case he made too much noise. He went round to the front of the house and peered in at each window.

There was only one man. It took a while for Bill's eyes to adjust to the lack of light, but as he craned up to see through the broken panes of the window, the small glow of the cigar kept moving like a tiny beacon as the smoker rocked gently back and forth in the chair that had originally been on the porch.

He was a big fellow with several weeks' growth of beard on his broad, dark face. A shotgun lay across his knees as he sprawled in a contented way with both feet resting on the floor and gently easing the chair in a calming rhythm.

Bill stood silently in the dark. He had to

consider his position. The man was not alert, but a shotgun at close range was a deadlier weapon than a Colt .44, and even the poorest of shots could do brutal work with it in a confined space.

He heard a slight noise somewhere behind him and turned nervously, to see a small donkey looking at him over a low fence. It was in the corral where Helen McCourt would have kept her horse, and was probably the animal's companion. Bill looked at it for a moment while a slight grin came over his face.

He went quietly round to the gate of the corral and let the little animal out. It moved willingly, happy to have company again. He led it gently round to the back door of Jesse Clark's house, up the two wooden steps into the narrow kitchen and through to the passage. Then he gave it a wallop on its rump and withdrew into the kitchen again.

The animal could be heard blundering along the floorboards amid a burst of swearing and noise of footsteps and a door opening violently. Bill looked out from behind the kitchen door. He caught a glimpse of the large man coming out of the room, to find himself up against the flank of a bewildered donkey. The man started pushing at it with the shotgun and was too occupied to notice the dark figure that suddenly appeared behind him. Bill's Colt hit him across the side of the head and the man fell to his knees. He dropped the shotgun with a loud clatter.

The donkey wandered along the corridor, nosed its way through the open front door, and stumbled down the steps of the house into the lane. Bill looked at his opponent. The man was bleeding from a shallow head-wound and breathed heavily as he lay in the dust. It was the work of a moment to gather up shotgun and pistol before racing up the stairs to the room where the packet lay beneath the stone slabs.

Although it was dark, Bill knew exactly where he was going. He was kneeling in front of the stove a moment or two later. He pulled out his knife and dug furiously around the slabs. One of them moved easily and he thrust it savagely to one side.

His hand found the slippery surface of an oiled-silk packet, tied with thick string.

SEVEN

Bill Hardman rode back to the cabin with a feeling that the worst was over. He hoped that the little man would return there early so that they could get away before someone started trying to find them. The moon was out now, throwing long shadows but marking the trail enough for a steady trot.

The little canyon was like a black hole in the dark slopes that rose from the surrounding land. He slowed down as he entered it, letting his mount pick its way among the pebbles and low bushes which littered the path. He was feeling almost elated at the prospect of the long journey back to Mexico. The little packet was safely in his saddlebag and he was well clear of the feuds in Santa Rosa.

He drew rein outside the little cabin and loosened the girth of his horse before tethering it near some tufts of grass that would keep it occupied until it went off to sleep for a while. He entered the hut, pushing the door noisily back on its rusty hinges and taking out his little copper Vesta box as he neared the table.

He struck a light and found himself staring into the barrels of two pistols.

'Don't do anythin' silly,' a man's voice said with soft menace. 'I ain't figurin' to kill nobody, fella, but I ain't takin' me no risks with a professional gun-handler.'

'I'm not takin' risks either,' Bill said as calmly as he could. 'Shall I light the candle? It's right there on the table.'

'You do that, then we can see what we've caught.'

Bill Hardman applied the Vesta to the thick

candle-stub which sat in the centre of the rough planks. It threw a warm glow across the little space and he could make out the features of the man in front of him. He could also see the figure of Helen McCourt as she held the other Colt with a steady hand. It was the same gun she had used last time they met. An old Navy weapon with the hammer pulled back ready for action.

'I wasn't expectin' visitors,' Bill said quietly. 'Where's Pete Willet?'

'Still waitin' for me.' Helen smiled. 'I'm not fool enough to go trailin' out to Parvo Creek and leave Jesse's house unguarded. You've been there, fella?'

Bill Hardman was doing some quick thinking. The man who stood at Helen's side was short and thickset. His eyes were narrowed as though he had trouble working things out, and his mouth moved as he chewed a plug of tobacco.

'I went out there,' Bill admitted with a grin. 'And got what I went for, too.'

His opponents looked at each other and a

flash of triumph seemed to pass between them. Helen McCourt leaned forward eagerly.

'Where is it?' she demanded urgently.

'In my saddle-bag.'

'Go get it, Harry–' She stopped in mid-sentence as though realizing that she could not trust her companion. 'No, I'll go for it.' she said sharply. 'You just keep an eye on this fella.'

She left the hut and Bill Hardman spread his hands wide as a gesture of defeat.

'I suppose you'll divide it between you,' he said sadly. 'It's certainly too much money for one fella.'

'How much?' The man's voice was eager.

'Well, I ain't counted it and I only have Jesse's word to go on, but there's reckoned to be seven thousand dollars in one packet and ten thousand in the other. Which one will you get?'

The man was licking his lips as he turned his head slightly towards the door as if in anticipation.

'Do you reckon she'll come back?' Bill asked innocently. 'Seventeen thousand dollars is one hell of a temptation.'

The man looked uncertainly at Bill Hardman before moving across to the window and pushing the piece of sacking aside. Before he could glance out into the night the door creaked open and Helen McCourt entered the cabin, holding the package. She was flushed as she waved it at her relieved companion. Her gun had been thrust into the waist of her skirt and she crossed to the table to let the candlelight fall on the oiled-silk trophy.

'We've got it, Harry,' she crooned in the flickering light. 'We've got Jesse's poke.'

Bill Hardman said nothing. He was watching the man's face and could see the hardening of expression as Harry's slow mind took in the fact that only one packet was being delivered.

'Where's the other one?' the man asked hoarsely.

Helen McCourt looked at him. 'What

other one?' she asked.

Bill Hardman laughed. 'I told you she'd do it, Harry,' he said cheerfully. 'It's one hell of a temptation.'

'What in hell's name are you two talkin' about?' Helen demanded to know.

'Where did you hide the other packet?' Bill asked. 'Harry thinks you're cheatin' on him.'

There was a tense silence as she looked from one man to the other.

'There was only one packet out there,' she said slowly as her hand reached down towards the gun. 'This fella's been givin' you a run-around, Harry. I wouldn't cheat an old friend.'

Her voice was urgent and contained a note of sincerity that was meant to soothe while her fingers felt for the butt of the Navy Colt. It was Bill Hardman's turn to move. He made a sudden dive for the floor.

'She's goin' for her gun, Harry!' he yelled.

The startled man did not know which enemy to meet first. His gun wavered for a moment between Bill Hardman and the woman with whom he was supposed to be working. He saw the movement of her right hand and lashed out with the barrel of his pistol. It caught her across the side of the head and she reeled back against the wooden wall with a cry of pain. The packet fell to the floor and, as the man stooped to pick it up, Bill Hardman pushed the table against his legs.

Harry stumbled to his knees, but managed to spin round to face the attack. He raised the Colt but the table moved again and his aim was upset as he staggered to regain his feet. Bill Hardman's gun was out, and before Harry could recover his balance, the noise of the shot filled the little cabin to send him falling backwards on the dirt floor. He moved a little before lying still in front of the girl he had just attacked.

She was on her feet now, holding the side of her face where blood trickled to stain the high collar of her gingham dress. Bill Hardman reached over and took the gun from her waist. He then picked up the package from the floor and stuffed it into his shirt. He waited patiently for her to recover her poise.

'You lose, Helen,' he said as she moved slowly to one of the rough chairs and sat down. 'Where are your horses?'

She looked at him with hatred on her dark face.

'At the far end of the canyon,' she said angrily. 'You might have got me killed back there, fella.'

'I might at that,' he admitted. 'If it was a choice between you and me, lady, it'd be you every time. And don't ever forget that.'

'I won't.' She took out a large white bandanna from her sleeve to hold against her damaged face. 'Did you kill Dave as well?' she asked quietly.

'Dave? The fella in town? Was that his name? No, he's just got a slightly bigger headache than you'll have. Dave wasn't very bright.'

She managed a smile.

'He wasn't meant to be. I figured you'd

expect somebody to be on guard, and that you'd get the money one way or another. Dave wasn't bright enough to stop you. But then you'd come back here, and we'd be waiting.'

'Smart lady. And you knew about this cabin, of course?'

'Of course. I suggested this place to Jesse a few years ago. Always handy if trouble starts. My pa used it durin' the gold days. So, what happens now?'

'So now you go back to town.'

She looked at the body on the floor and eyed the two guns that Bill Hardman held.

'What about my pa's gun?' she asked with a final show of defiance.

Bill grinned. 'I'm hangin' on to that,' he told her. 'Little ladies who keep pointin' guns at folk don't get to keep them. And you're walkin' home, ma'am, so a gun would be a heavy thing to tote all that way.'

'Walking?' Her voice rose in pitch and she almost screamed the word.

He nodded. 'It's easy. You just go out that

door and head south. I'll unharness the horses and turn 'em loose. They'll find their own way home. Might even make it before you do. Now get moving.'

He waved her father's gun at her and she knew that there was no arguing the point. She delivered an unladylike curse as she left the cabin and began walking down the canyon, picking her way carefully in the moonlight. Bill Hardman watched from the doorway until she was out of sight. Then he went back to the cabin to pick up Harry's gun. He shoved it into his belt and returned to the canyon to run to the northern end, where Helen McCourt's little buggy was across the trail while the horse between the shafts nibbled at some low bushes. Harry's mount was there as well, tethered to the buggy and dozing fitfully.

Bill Hardman removed the saddle from the riding animal, released the other horse from the shafts of the buggy, and gave them both a sharp smack across their rumps to send them galloping out of the north end of the canyon. He was smiling contentedly as he walked back to the cabin.

The stub was spluttering now and he searched the little room for another source of lighting. There were two more candles on a small shelf and he lit one of them from the flickering piece. The place grew brighter as he pulled the package from his shirt and placed it on the table for examination.

He had not forgotten the promise he had made to the Pinkerton man. He would check that the little packet contained nothing but money. His sharp pocket knife made a careful slit in one end of the oiled-silk wrapping. He prised the covering back a little and could see the edges of the dollar bills. He nodded his contentment as he pushed the gap closed and then poured some hot wax from the candle across the slit to seal and make it waterproof again. He rubbed some dirt across the cooling wax and the package looked almost as though it had not been tampered with.

Satisfied with his work, Bill lit the stove

and placed the coffee-pot on top of it. He went out to his own horse to get some food from the saddlebags and set about making himself a much-needed meal.

Pete would still be on the trail back from Parvo Creek and it could be another hour or so before he reached the cabin. He might even lie up somewhere for the night. He would certainly be a worried little man.

Bill Hardman could not risk going to sleep. His own horse was right outside the cabin and there was always a chance that Helen McCourt might double back to steal it. He took the heavy wooden chair and went to sit in the doorway with the hot cup of coffee in his hand while a plate of bacon and beans sat on his knee. His horse looked at him as though puzzled by the strange actions. Then it turned its attention to the grassy patches and ignored its owner.

He eventually dozed. It was a fitful sort of sleep, disturbed by the movements of the animal or by slipping from his own position on the rough chair.

He was jerked awake by the sound of hoofbeats on the gravel at the southern end of the canyon. Little Pete Willet was returning at last. Bill got up from his chair, went into the cabin and lit the candle. He poked at the fire in the stove and placed the coffee-pot on top to heat up again. He was looking forward to a bit of company on the long journey back across the border. The prospect of so much money for such an easy job brought a slight smile to his face.

It was wiped off when the door swung open. The man who stood there was not Pete Willet. He was a big man, unshaven and unwashed, with a vivid scar across the side of his head where Bill Hardman had hit him in Jesse Clark's house.

EIGHT

Dave Morland blinked in the light and stared for a moment at the last person he was expecting to meet. His brother's body lay on the floor in a pool of drying blood, and the man who stood in front of him was the one who had been pointed out by Helen McCourt as a messenger for Jesse Clark. The man who had hit him and left him nearly unconscious.

He recovered from the momentary shock and went for the gun at his side. His hands were large and clumsy, and before the weapon was properly out of its holster, Bill Hardman had picked up the old Navy Colt from the table and cocked it.

'Don't do anythin' silly, fella,' the younger man said in a flat voice, 'Just keep your hands well away from trouble.'

'That's my brother you killed there,' Dave Morland growled huskily. He looked round the cabin. 'Where's Miss McCourt?' he asked in bewilderment.

'She left.'

'You killed her too?'

'No.' Bill Hardman shook his head. 'She's walkin' home. You must have missed her on the trail. So, tell me what you're doin' here, fella. This cabin seems to be mighty popular all of a sudden.'

Dave Morland licked his lips nervously.

'I came lookin' for them,' he said. 'They was due back after...'

'After killin' me?'

'I guess so.'

'If you hadn't killed me in Santa Rosa.'

'No.' The man shook his head violently. 'I weren't goin' to kill you, fella. You was the only one who knew where the money was hid. I had to play like some blue-belly sentry. You was supposed to think I was really guardin' the place, and I was to let you get the packet and high-tail it back here.

And they'd be waiting.'

Bill shook his head in reluctant admiration.

'You took a risk,' he said. 'I might have killed you.'

The man grinned a little.

'Well, you sure as hell gave me a real pounding. But Helen said you was some gentlemanlike fella who didn't go around shootin' folks.' He looked down at his brother's body. 'Unless you had to.'

Dave Morland was still glancing round the cabin. His enemy had another gun stuck in his belt and a third one in his holster. It looked as if every move Dave made would be easily countered. He knew that the gun held by Bill Hardman belonged to Helen McCourt and that it was as dangerous as any modern pistol in the right hands. He found himself sweating in the confined space as he moved away very slightly so that his back was against the door.

It was still partially open and he had some vague idea of suddenly diving through it and hoping to pull out his Colt at the same time.

'Unbuckle your belt.'

The words took him by surprise and he hesitated for a moment before reaching down with nervous fingers. Before he could do anything, something hit him in the back and he pitched forward almost as far as the table. Someone had flung open the door and Dave Morland could only try to save himself as he stumbled. He could see Bill Hardman's legs at the other side of the table. The young man had jumped back and Dave saw his chance of escape.

He went for his gun and pulled it swiftly from the holster. The hammer came back easily under his anxious finger as he grabbed the edge of the table with his other hand to lever himself up to a firing position. Then something hit him across the back of the head and he slumped forward, catching his chin on the edge of the table. The gun went off as his finger clutched spasmodically at the trigger. A little spray of dirt rose from the earthen floor as the bullet ploughed harmlessly into it. Then Dave Morland died from the gaping gash across the back of his head.

Pete Willet stood in the open doorway. He still held the shotgun in his trembling hands and was looking at the blood on the stock as if it were some horrible apparition.

'Have I killed him?' he asked nervously.

'You sure have, and just in time to stop him killin' me,' Bill said with a relieved grin.

'I saw his horse out there and wondered what the hell was going on.' Pete looked at the other corpse. 'I reckon as how you've had a busy time, fella,' he said in an attempt to sound light-hearted. 'She never turned up, Bill. I waited and waited, but the damned bitch never showed.'

'She showed all right.'

Bill told him what had happened. The two men pulled the bodies out of the cabin and dragged them behind a clump of bushes. They returned to the hut where Pete Willet took a welcome mug of coffee while they made their plans for moving out.

It was not considered safe to spend the rest of the night in the canyon. Although it was only a few hours to dawn and the moon had already gone down, Bill decided it was best to leave before Helen McCourt had a chance to return with more help. He found, to his surprise that there was a lot more to Pete Willet than he had imagined. The little man had a quick grasp of what was needed for their safe journey.

He produced from under the tattered bed a large parcel of used clothes and old cooking utensils. They smelled of damp and a few 'roaches crawled away from the stuff as it was piled in the centre of the floor. Bill looked on in mild amusement as the little man packed the items into two old sacks, ready to be loaded on Helen McCourt's buggy.

'What are we takin' that stuff with us for?' he asked.

Pete Willet gave him a sly grin.

'Jesse and me has done deals across the border more than once. Sellin' old clothes is as good a reason to travel as any. There are plenty of poor folks down in Mexico who'll buy stuff we'd throw away. Border patrols and nosy lawmen don't bother a trader in old clothes. Besides, who'd want to search through this lot? There's more than just a few 'roaches in there.'

Bill Hardman could easily believe it.

'Have you got a horse to pull the buggy?' he asked.

'My old mare will do that. She's used to drawin' Jesse's rig from time to time. Don't worry, lad, I'll get you safely to Mexico without them army fellas botherin' you. You got the money safe?'

Bill nodded and patted his shirt.

'Quite safe,' he said.

'Then there's another trick me and Jesse has up our sleeves.'

Pete grinned as he picked up an old iron kettle that stood by the pot-bellied stove. It was a large article, slightly rusty, and with a long snout that had a little chip knocked out of it. He placed it proudly on the table.

Bill Hardman watched as the little man wrestled with the tight lid before tipping the kettle over so that the inside could be seen clearly in the soft candlelight.

'Notice anything'?' he asked.

Bill looked into the kettle and was almost going to say that he could see nothing unusual when he suddenly realized that there was no hole for hot water to be poured from the spout. He glanced at Pete's grinning face as the little man put the lid back on.

'You can fill that kettle with water,' he said, 'and put in any sealed packet. Then just let it stand in front of the fire with a drop of water added to the spout. The spout heats up, gives off steam, and no fella is goin' to be bothered lookin' into a boilin' kettle.'

'Jesse had this specially made?' Bill asked in admiration.

'Sure did. Twenty years ago. We've moved a few little things back and forth since then, and nobody has ever looked into a boilin' kettle.'

'Yeah, but what if somebody wanted to use

the water to make coffee?'

'You make sure you have another can of water on the fire. Jesse thought it all out and had this thing made by a fella back in Phoenix. So here's what you do. If we get followed by the law or them blue-bellies, we slip the packet into the kettle. Then fill it and the spout with water. We start a fire as if we was settlin' down for a meal, and you just place it where the water in the spout will start steaming. It works every time.'

'You and Jesse Clark are surely one connivin' pair,' Bill said with a laugh.

'Ain't we just?' chuckled Pete as he made for the door. 'I'll put my horse to the buggy and we'll be outa here in an hour or less. We'll clear this place out. I don't intend comin' back here with two dead bodies stinkin' up the canyon and Helen McCourt on my tail.'

Bill looked round the cabin. There did not seem to be anything worth taking with them, but he figured that what was rubbish to him, might be precious to Pete Willet. He went to the door to tighten the girth on his horse and pile the sacks outside ready for departure.

There was a keen wind blowing along the canyon as the two men set out an hour before dawn. Pete Willet drove the buggy with the cotton seat-covers removed to make it look less conspicuous. The sacks of smelly clothes and cooking utensils were piled behind him with his saddle and the old shotgun, which was the only weapon he owned.

Bill Hardman rode alongside with the comforting feel of Jesse Clark's money tightly wedged under his shirt. They had released Dave Morland's horse to find its own way home. Pete had wanted to take it with them, but Bill Hardman had no intention of being accused of stealing by some travelling lawman who might recognize the brand.

Pete knew the route that had to be followed: to travel west for a few hours so that Santa Rosa could be given a wide berth, and then turn south to travel, as Bill had done on his journey, to make for the old mission of Tumacacori. Pete Willet had a contact there at the temporary army camp, which was responsible for sending out regular cavalry patrols. The death of Colonel Barstin's wife had created so much activity that it would be difficult to slip through the net without some knowledge of where the patrols were active.

They travelled slowly through the morning as the clouds cleared from the peaks of the mountains and the air grew warm again as the wind dropped. Stops had to be carefully calculated to reach a place where water was to be found for the night. Creeks were few and far apart for travellers who were not sticking to well-established routes.

Pete Willet led the way with the ease born of long experience of the wide emptiness that lay ahead of them. They stopped for the first night at a pool that was fed by an underground stream. The water was tepid and bitter, but acceptable to thirsty men and horses.

They reached the old mission building of Tumacacori by late afternoon the next day. It stood as a forlorn reminder of a grander past. It's red-tinged frontage was scoured by the winds that came off the mountains, and birds nested around the fallen roof. There were tents pitched just beyond it, some two dozen of them in neat rows with soldier-boys moving about near the horse lines.

A Mexican cantina of rough adobe lay slightly to the west of that, surrounded by a few poor houses and some corrals.

'Don't forget our story,' Pete Willet said as they drew up outside the cantina. 'You and me is goin' down to Mexico to do some trading. We'll take a drink in here to show that we ain't stand-offish, and then pitch camp just beyond the creek back of the mission. The soldier-boys might get curious, and they might even search us. So just play it cool, fella, and don't look like some hired gun on the prod.'

Bill Hardman glanced around. He was

nervous about being among so many people.

'We could have bypassed this place,' he said in a dubious voice.

'Can't be done. One of these blue-bellies is my contact. He'll tell us where the patrols are likely to be in the morning. The border is only about ten or twelve miles south of here, and by this time tomorrow we'll be well on our way to Jesse's place.'

They went into the small cantina, took a couple of glasses of the cloudy beer, and then went to set up their camp behind the damaged walls of the old mission. The creek was narrow, with thick grass along its edges. The water was clear and the fried bacon tasted as good as it smelt. Pete Willet got to his feet after a while and held out his hand.

'Give me five dollars,' he said abruptly.

Bill Hardman looked at him and the little man grinned.

'He don't talk 'cos he likes me,' he said. 'These fellas don't get paid worth a damn, and passin' on a bit of news can earn them the price of a few drinks. This fella I'm meetin' is stuck out here for months on end. He's been useful to Jesse a few times, but he don't give nothin' for free.'

Bill reached into his waistcoat pocket and produced five silver coins. The little man took them and strolled back towards the cantina. Bill Hardman settled down by the fire, rested his head on a saddle, and began to doze.

Then he remembered the possibility of some officious soldier coming along to check on the strangers. He looked carefully around in the darkness before taking the package from his shirt and placing it in the large iron kettle that lay near the fire. He filled it with water and then poured some more down the long spout. He put the heavy utensil close enough to the fire so that only a slight push would place the spout near the flames and cause the water in it to boil. That done, he felt that he could drop off to sleep with a clear conscience.

Bill did not remember what woke him, but it was a sudden thing that brought him instantly alert. He reached for the gun at his side almost as his eyes opened in the fading firelight. A group of shadowy figures stood around him. They were silhouetted by the flames but he could see the glint of weapons in their hands and the darkness of their Indian faces.

NINE

'Don't try anythin' silly, fella.' The voice was harsh and belonged to a short, thickset man who squeezed between two of the Indians. He carried a shotgun in his large hands and his swarthy face glowed in the firelight. He was not dressed like a cowpoke, but more like some city fellow with a dark frock-coat and doeskin waistcoat below which was a broad gunbelt that housed a Colt.

Bill Hardman stood up slowly, his hands only inches above his own gun as he did so.

'And who the hell are you?' he asked.

The man came nearer. He was clean-shaven, with a thin mouth and large, fleshy nose that bore a slight scar.

'Bert Ebdon told me about you,' he said in a hostile voice. 'I bin kinda hopin' you'd show up somewhere around here.'

Bill breathed a sigh of relief. Another Pinkerton man was hardly anything to worry about. His fingers relaxed.

'Yes,' he said. 'I met Bert on the other side of the border. I guess you're checkin' up on me.'

The man nodded. 'You might say that,' he conceded.

Bill waved a hand towards the silent circle of Indians.

'These fellas belong to you?' he asked.

'Yeah. They sorta guard my back. Did you pick up the money you was supposed to be collecting?'

'Yes. And I checked it, as Bert asked me to. It is only money. Nothin' more interestin' than that.'

The man gave a mean grin. 'Only money,' he repeated. 'Well, it may only be money to you and Bert, fella, but it's the best thing in the world to me. I'll take it now.'

Bill looked hard at the man. He was not joking. The shotgun had been levelled and the Indians were also firmly pointing their old Spencers at their quarry.

'And what makes you think I haven't already passed it on?' he asked. 'If I was carryin' all that cash money, I'd be goin' around with some protection. Just like you. I thought all Pinkerton fellas were honest.'

The man advanced to within a couple of feet.

'You got more money tucked away than I can earn in ten years, so just pass it over and we can part without no shootin' to disturb folks.'

'The army are only a coupla hoots and a holler away,' Bill pointed out. 'They might get curious if there was any shooting.'

'I'm a Pinkerton man and these fellas is my scouts. If I come across a wanted hold-up fella who resists arrest, I figure as how I'd have to shoot him in self-defence. That's reasonable, ain't it?'

'I see your point. Well, if you don't believe I've passed on the money, make a search.'

Bill Hardman brushed past the man to kneel down in front of the fire. He placed an enamel water-container over the flames, and at the same time moved the kettle closer to the heat so that the spout was almost in the burning wood. He sat back casually against his saddle and waited to see what would happen next.

The Pinkerton man gave orders to the Indians in some language that Bill Harman had never heard. They scrambled around the little camp, throwing blankets and saddles aside, turning out the contents of the sacks, and grabbing Bill so that they could search him. He submitted meekly and watched with studied calm as they explored the buggy and opened the saddle-bags.

The enamel container soon heated up and Bill began to make himself a cup of coffee.

The kettle also appeared to be boiling as steam rose from the spout and he moved it casually away from the heat.

He watched as the Indians reported to their boss that they had found nothing. The Pinkerton man was beginning to look a little uncertain. He stared from right to left in an agitated manner before letting his narrowed eyes rest on the two grazing horses that stood over by the buggy.

'There were two of you,' he snarled. 'There was a little fella with you. Where is he now?'

'Gone to report to the military.'

The man stared. It was not the answer he expected.

'Why would he do that?, he asked.

'They got an interest in that packet, as well as you,' Bill replied with a certain malicious satisfaction. 'And they want to be sure that money is all we're carrying. He's meetin' now with the boss fella who'll be a witness to what we're carryin' and who it's handed to. Our job's finished. You're too late.'

The Pinkerton man stood silently for a moment, taking in the meaning of what he was being told. Then he suddenly came over to Bill, dragged him to his feet, and pushed him back against the wall of the old mission. The cup of coffee had flown from Bill's hand and the other man had cast aside the shotgun as he grappled with his victim.

'So who in hell's got the money now?' he yelled in a desperate voice. 'Give me a name or I'll put a bullet through you.'

'You're not killin' anybody, fella,' Bill said in a low voice. 'My gun is pressin' against your belly and I'd be happy to use it.'

The Pinkerton man looked down just as the barrel of Bill's Colt poked him just under the waistcoat. He loosed one hand from the young man's throat to go for his own gun, but it was too late. Bill's left hand had already reached out and removed it from the holster to let it drop to the ground.

'You got too eager, fella,' Bill Hardman said quietly. 'Now, tell your Indians to go peddle their wares. If anythin' happens to me, it'll sure as hell happen to you.'

The man hesitated for a second and then shouted something angrily to the circle of motionless men. They did not respond for a moment and Bill began to think that his bluff was being called. Then they quietly faded beyond the rays of the flickering firelight and he and the Pinkerton man seemed to be alone.

'You're a right sensible fella,' Bill said in a normal voice.

'So what happens now?' the man asked.

'You sit down at the other side of the fire, and we wait until my partner gets back. You make a wrong move, and I'll kill you.'

The man gulped noisily.

'And when he gets back?' he asked.

Bill grinned as he pushed the man in the belly to propel him away from the wall.

'Then we march a crooked Pinkerton man over to the soldier-boys and leave him to be delivered to the nearest marshal. You're in real trouble, fella.'

The man's mouth tightened. 'We could do

a deal,' he said urgently.

'With all them Indians back of you? No way that I can think of. We'll just let the army handle it.'

'Look, I was out to make me a few dollars. Nobody got hurt and them Indian fellas will go back to their pueblo a couple of miles north of here. I got somethin' to deal with. Somethin' I'll wager Bert Ebdon didn't tell you. Interested?'

'Keep talking.'

The man leaned forward across the fire. His face was a reddish hue as he spoke.

'Bert wanted to be sure that you was only carryin' money across the border to that fella, Jesse Clark. He was worried you might be carryin' somethin' else. Somethin' one hell of a lot more precious than a few thousand dollars.'

Bill Hardman tried to control his voice. 'And what would that be?' he asked.

'Have we got a deal? I tell you what it is, and you let me walk out of here?'

'If I think you're tellin' the truth.'

'Fair enough.' The man took a deep breath. 'I reckon my job with Pinkerton's is over, so here's what I know. Colonel Barstin's wife was carryin' somethin' more than just the usual trinkets of jewellery a woman like her would have. She had a packet of emeralds worth every cent of fifty thousand dollars. And she didn't come by 'em too honestly.'

'And that's what was stolen in the hold-up?'

'It sure was. They belonged to her mother, and when the old lady died, the emeralds went missin' and the family was real put out. One of the servants was blamed at first, but then her sisters reckoned as how she made off with them. She was travellin' south to meet up with her husband at Fort Grant when the hold-up took place. Her and the black girl was killed and the emeralds took. Colonel Barstin wants them back and he's got all the blue-bellies in the area huntin' for the killers. But he don't want us Pinkerton fellas findin' 'em first, and handin' 'em over to Mrs Barstin's sisters.'

'The killers could be any place. Why concentrate on the border?'

'Some farmin' folk saw them travellin' south and they was on Mexican saddles. The nearest marshal put the news out on the telegraph and the colonel had patrols out real pronto. So did all the local lawmen when they heard about the reward he was offering. It makes sense because stuff like that can only be sold in some big city and there ain't a place on this side of the border that it'd be safe to use right now. The colonel and the lawmen reckon that those emeralds is headin' for some place like Mexico City or Vera Cruz. There's dealers there.'

Bill nodded slowly. 'And the family is employin' Pinkerton to get to them first?'

The man gave a crooked grin. 'They don't aim to let the colonel cheat them out of their inheritance, fella. If he lays hands on the stuff, he'll likely do what the killers is tryin' to do. Get 'em over the border to the big dealers who'll take 'em out of their settings so that they can never be recognized again.

There's big money involved, fella. Real big money.'

Bill Hardman thought it over. It had a ring of truth and he was glad that he had checked the packet carefully. Everything the man said was making sense.

'I reckon you can take a walk,' he said.

'My gun?'

'That stays here. Just go collect your horse and get outa sight. I'll report to the army that you gave me the slip. You'd better keep out of their way.'

The man stood up, looked longingly at the pistol that still lay by the wall of the ruined mission, and then slowly walked into the darkness towards the little group of distant camp fires and crude tents that littered the area. Bill Hardman poured himself another cup of coffee.

It was twenty minutes or so later that Pete Willet returned. The little man took a mug of hot coffee with eager hands before telling his news. His fingers were trembling around the enamel cup as he drank, and his face was pale in the firelight.

'You all right, fella?' Bill asked anxiously.

'Fine, fine,' the little man replied. 'Just too much to drink, I guess. I got a list of tomorrow's patrols. We ought to move out now to get a start on them. These army fellas set off early in the mornings. They don't hang about.'

'I had visitors,' Bill Hardman said quietly.

'Yeah?'

'Yeah. And I got me a feelin' that you saw 'em.'

Pete Willet grinned slyly. 'Well, I ain't no hero,' he admitted, 'so I sorta hung back to see what happened. You managed right well without me.'

'I could have been killed, Pete. What would you have done then?'

'I had my plans,' the little man protested. 'If things had gotten rough, I'd have gone back to the cantina and got my army contact to come back with a few other blue-bellies. They'd have finished anythin' them Indians started.'

'It's nice to know I was safe,' Bill said drily.

'I just waited to see what happened. The less them soldier fellas know, the better. We don't want no fuss, do we?'

'Yeah, you got a point there, and that kettle certainly worked a treat. Let's get movin' then.'

They began packing their gear and harnessing the horses. As they worked, Bill noticed that there were some bloodstains on Pete Willet's sleeve. He glanced at the scabbarded knife the little man carried behind his right hip. There were also stains round the belt and on his pants.

He then recalled that while he was drinking his coffee and waiting, there had been a sort of strangled cry from somewhere in the darkness. He now had a feeling that a crooked Pinkerton man had not managed to reach his horse.

TEN

They travelled through the dawn in a south-westerly direction before turning due south towards the mountains and deep valleys that lay between. Pete Willet had a list of all the patrols the army were sending out for the next few days. He was leading Bill Hardman away from the areas where soldiers would be likely to appear.

They kept a sharp look-out as the sun rose and the mist cleared on the high ground. Pete assured his companion that the military would not yet be about and their first patrols would be moving more to the east along the flatter trails.

The kettle was packed away in the buggy. It had served its purpose once and might be useful again. There was still water in it, and if they spotted any patrols in the distance, they would at once stop as if to camp, light a fire, and place the kettle near it.

Bill Hardman was nervous. He had a feeling that if the crooked Pinkerton man was dead, the Indian scouts might be looking for the killer. He decided to ask Pete Willet very bluntly if he had knifed the man.

The little fellow was not offended by the question. He just shrugged and gave a wide grin.

'And you don't have to worry about them Indians,' he said as if sensing the next question. 'If the soldier-boys find that fella's body, they'll see that he's been scalped, neat as neat. Them Indians will be too busy runnin' back to their pueblo to bother poor folk like us.'

'Pueblo Indians don't scalp folk,' Bill said testily.

Pete threw back his head in derision. 'Them soldier-boys don't know that,' he chuckled. 'They think all Indians go around scalpin' folk. They know that the Pinkerton fella was hirin' Indian scouts, so I reckon as how they'll be usin' some of their patrols to hunt them down.'

They rode on silently for a while, watching the horizon carefully and stopping for a meal near a sluggish creek that came down cold from the distant hills.

'How far to the border?' Bill asked as they ate.

'Just nine miles if we turn south in the next hour or so. There's a narrow trail between them two hills. The blue-bellies won't use it because it don't give them a good sight of the surroundin' area. They always like to be on the high ground when they're patrolling. That's goin' to give us about five miles travellin' out of sight of anybody.'

He looked sharply at Bill Hardman. 'It ain't the soldiers as worries me,' he said. 'It's the McCourt woman. She wants that money real bad. Her and Jesse was close and she knows where he's hidin' out now. The damned woman knows too much about his business, and she thinks he let her down by not leavin' some cash money for her before he took off.'

'From what I hear, he didn't have time.'

'He sure as hell didn't. The whole thing blew up like a keg of gunpowder. I still haven't figured it out. One minute, he's got the town all tamed and doin' as he says. Next minute – they want to lynch him.'

'How did it start?'

The little man thought about it for a moment. 'Well, I was in the saloon that night, helpin' Matt tap some beer-barrels ready for business. Then two of the Morland brothers come in and go to watch a faro game over in the corner. Somebody says somethin' about bad luck, and the next minute, the Morland brothers are talkin' of a crooked game. Matt goes over and they start beatin' the hell outa him. I made myself scarce through the back door.'

He licked his lips nervously at the memory. 'Next thing that happens is that Ma Pendry comes into town on a wagon and starts complainin' to the marshal that Jesse cheated her on the farm deal. Well, of course he cheated. That's Jesse's way. Next minute, the marshal is surrounded by folks all sayin' that Jesse should be run outa town. It was as though the whole thing was bein' planned.'

Bill nodded. 'Sounds as if it was,' he agreed. 'How did Helen McCourt figure in it?'

'I reckon she was behind it. She stood on the corner of the street with the banker and the mayor. I'll swear to hell that they tipped the nod to the marshal to go raid the saloon and close down the gambling. It was all like they'd planned it. Somebody started throwin' stones through the windows, Matt and the two barmen got the hell out like I did, and the folks took over the place. Then they bust open Jesse's gun store and began emptyin' it. I was scared, fella. Real scared.'

He poured himself more coffee and took a sip of the scalding liquid.

'I reckon that the McCourt woman told the Morlands that Jesse was due back in town that night. They high-tailed it outa

Santa Rosa, so I got to horse and rode out as well. I figured to try and meet up with Jesse before they did.'

'And you met up with him?'

'Sure did, and he was able to get away to Mexico. They were out to kill him that night.'

'So a lotta folks profited by Jesse's departure,' Bill Hardman mused.

Pete thought about it. 'Well, they emptied his store and they've got his saloon. His house has been looted bare, and all the folk who owe him money don't have to pay it back. I suppose you're right on that one. And Ma Pendry might be able to get her farm back as well as keep the money she was paid for it. I reckon that banker fella will do well out of it too. He had a few deals goin' with Jesse that didn't show on his books. There's a little cash money lyin' around that bank that don't have to be accounted for.'

Bill looked hard at his companion. 'And you stayed loyal,' he said in a neutral voice.

The man grinned again. 'Oh, sure. I'm a

real honest, upright sort of fella,' he said. 'There's things you don't know, Bill, but Jesse and me is kin. His pa was quite a travellin' man but he never did get around to marryin' my ma. Jesse got all his pa's money, and his pa's ideas of how to make more. I just tagged along. And Jesse always looked after me. I'm no hero, Bill, but I stick with Jesse the way he stuck with me.'

He paused for a moment and closed his eyes. 'But I can't say I won't run for cover when things get dangerous,' he added in a shamefaced way. He opened his eyes again and looked at Bill Hardman. 'I suppose you're wonderin' if I'll come up behind you like I did with that Pinkerton fella? Well, I won't. My job is to get you and that packet to Jesse. I ain't got the guts to do it myself, so you're as safe with me as if you was back home in bed. Jesse knows me, Bill. I got nothin' without him.'

'So what's our next move?'

'We go along that valley and come out bearing slightly east. There's a small town

135

there named Wryton. The Mexicans call it La Parada because it's the last stop on this side of the border. I've got another contact there and he might be able to tell me how active the Mexican patrols are over on their side. There's a town marshal but I don't trust him and he'll be suspicious of every stranger while they're on the look-out for Ma Barstin's killers. Everybody's offerin' rewards. We'd better camp out of town, and you stay with the horses while I go in and get the information. Make sure you place the packet in the kettle before we get within hollerin' distance of the place. I'd hate some small-town lawman to go spoilin' things now.'

'I wouldn't be too happy myself,' Bill said drily.

Wryton was an adobe town, spread on both sides of a small river. It lay on low ground at the base of the wooded hills and a slight haze hung above it from the cooking-fires. It seemed more Mexican than northern but had a brick-built jailhouse and a prominent bank next to a large general store. The telegraph wires crossed the valley on their slender poles and entered the town near the main street.

The two men looked down at the place from the height of the tree line. They were hot and tired, covered in trail dust and ready to make camp and eat. Pete suggested doing this within sight of the buildings so that they would appear less suspicious to the local lawman. They could build a fire, make a meal, and just wait to see if he paid them a visit.

There were a few men cutting trees on the lower slopes of the hills and they noted the presence of the strangers with interest. They quit work to return to the town about half an hour before sundown, hauling their timber with them on a large wagon drawn by two horses. The marshal came riding out shortly afterwards, heading for the little camp on a large black horse that travelled at a spanking pace over the rough ground. He had a deputy with him; their badges gleamed in the last of the sunlight.

Pete had already lit a fire and placed the kettle near it. The packet was safely inside and the spout was filled with water. He had broken out the food supplies and another pot bubbled above the flames with hot coffee giving up its strong scent as the two riders drew up and got down from their horses.

The marshal was a large man with massive sideburns of curly grey hair that stuck out from under the broad hat. He had a considerable paunch but looked tough enough as he strode towards the two strangers and glanced round at their little camp. His deputy was a younger man, tall and slim, who kept in the background and carried a shotgun in the crook of his arm.

'And who would you folks be?' the marshal asked in a dry, raspy voice. 'We don't get many strangers round this part of the world.'

Bill Hardman gave their real names and just mentioned that they were passing through on their way to Mexico. The lawman nodded as he listened, his sharp grey eyes taking in the scene.

'That's an interestin' rig you got there,' he said as he pointed to the buggy. 'More like somethin' a lady would be using.'

Pete Willet picked up the kettle with the aid of a piece of cloth. He seemed to find the handle too hot and put it down again.

'I'm takin' some used clothes and kitchen stuff to sell over the border,' the little man explained. 'Anythin' to make a living, Marshal.'

The lawman looked hard at Pete. 'I know you, don't I?' he asked as he screwed up his eyes in an effort to remember. 'Don't you work for Jesse Clark?'

Pete licked his lips. 'That's right,' he admitted, 'but he's in Mexico right now and I'm sellin' this stuff so that I can make enough cash to join him there.'

'Yeah, I bin hearin' stories about Jesse. Seems they kicked him outa Santa Rosa in a hurry. Now, I got me no quarrel with him, or with you, Pete.'

He turned to Bill Hardman. 'But you I ain't heard of, fella,' he said, 'save for a complaint from a Miss Helen McCourt back in Santa Rosa. Seems you did a bit of killin' in that town. Two fellas by the name of Morland.'

Bill Hardman was watching the marshal's right hand and also noting the deputy's position.

'They was tryin' to kill me,' he said quietly. 'It was a fair fight.'

'Maybe it was, maybe it weren't. That don't rightly concern me, but this Miss McCourt sent a message on the telegraph that says you stole her pa's old Navy Colt gun and her buggy. She reckons as how I oughta arrest you if you crosses my path. I can see the buggy, so where's the gun?'

'She tried to shoot me,' Bill Hardman said, 'and I had to take it off her.'

'Maybe so, but I gotta take you in until she comes to town and makes a formal charge. Or maybe she'll just be content to get the gun back again and save herself the trouble.

You'd better saddle up your horse and we'll head for town.'

'Shovin' me in jail, Marshal, seems a bit drastic for one gun.'

'And the buggy, fella. Don't forget that.'

'I guess not. And is she comin' all the way from Santa Rosa to appear in court?'

'Well, that's as may be,' the marshal grinned, 'but I gotta carry out the law. I'm not sayin' that you couldn't be released on a cash surety. Judge Byers ain't averse to a reasonable arrangement.'

He did not say who would benefit from the arrangement but Bill had little doubt what was in the lawman's mind. He turned to pick up the saddle for his horse, and as he did so, the marshal leaned forward, and extracted the gun from Bill's holster and stuck it in his own belt.

'Where is this Navy Colt?' the marshal asked.

'In my saddle-bags.'

The marshal nodded to his deputy. The young man picked up the worn leather pouches and emptied the contents on to the grass. The gun fell out and he retrieved it to hand over to his boss. The lawman examined it with a slight look of contempt on his rugged face before thrusting it into his belt with the other pistol.

'Don't seem to be worth makin' all this fuss about,' he said sadly. 'The buggy's worth more but she seems all het-up about an old gun.'

'Sentimental value, perhaps,' Bill suggested.

'You might be right, fella. Now, we got one more job to do before settin' off for town. A little matter of searchin' for some missin' jewellery.'

Bill grinned. 'I took her gun,' he said. 'Not her necklace.'

'Oh, it ain't her folderols I'm lookin' for,' the marshal said cheerfully, 'but we got orders from the army to search every stranger in case they got what was stole from Colonel Barstin's wife. There's a reward bein' offered, and I ain't takin' no chances of it slippin' me by. Go through everything, Charlie.'

Young Charlie did as he was told while Pete quietly poured out coffee and offered a mug of the steaming brew to the marshal. The lawman took it gratefully and stood blowing at it while his deputy searched the buggy and everything else in the little camp. Pete set down the coffee-pot and moved the kettle gently away from the fire. His gestures were born of experience and Bill stood admiring the spirit of the man.

'Nothin' here, boss,' young Charlie finally reported after he had searched Pete and Bill.

'Well, I reckon that completes our business then,' the marshal said in a slightly dis-appointed voice. 'Let's head back for town.'

Bill had already saddled his horse and Pete now stood up and began to gather the harness for his own animal. The marshal gestured him to stay where he was.

'Not you, fella,' he said brusquely. 'The lady didn't say nothin' about you in her message, so we don't aim to fill up the jailhouse more than we need. Just stay camped here until daylight. Then move on to wherever you're headed. Just don't come into town. There are one or two folk there who got no likin' for Jesse Clark, and I don't aim to have trouble on his account. And leave the buggy here. We'll send out for it in the morning.'

He motioned Bill Hardman to mount his horse while little Pete stood disconsolately as the three mounted men prepared for the ride back to Wryton.

ELEVEN

The cell was a small one, whitewashed and badly lit by only one tiny barred window which was set high in the wall. There was no glass to keep out the dust and smells, and the door of the cell opened straight into the

144

office of the marshal. There was another cell next to it, equally small, and apparently used to store various odds and ends which now included Bill Hardman's belongings.

The young prisoner lay on his narrow bunk, gazing up at the ceiling with its drab colouring and the inevitable tarantula in one corner, which served as a fly catcher. He watched the spider with interest. His experience of southern climes had told him that he was in no danger and that the creature was more interested in the local insect life than in human beings.

Two days had passed without anything happening. He had only fifteen dollars left of his expense money and had already offered it to the marshal. The man had been ready to accept, but then appeared to change his mind for some reason that Bill Hardman could not fathom.

His main worry was the packet that had been left with Pete at their campsite. He had not heard anything of the little man and did not want to show too much interest in his whereabouts to the marshal.

He was almost dropping off to sleep when the door of the office opened and the lawman entered with his heavy tread. He looked as if he had just enjoyed a good supper and was carrying a plate of bacon and beans for the prisoner. His deputy stood, as ever, just behind him as the cell door was opened a little to pass the food through. When the key was safely turned again, the deputy left the office and the marshal went to sit behind his battered desk.

'I got some news for you, fella,' he said in his raspy voice. 'The telegraph's bin goin' hell for leather this last day or so.'

Bill got up from the bed to cross to the barred door.

'Good news, I hope, Marshal,' he said hopefully.

The lawman grinned as he picked the last of his supper from his teeth.

'Well, that depends on how you look at it,' he said slowly. 'Good news for me, but bad news for you, I reckon.'

Bill Hardman waited silently. His hands were clutching the bars with a tight, spasmodic grip.

The marshal got up from the desk, went over to the pot-bellied stove, and poured a couple of mugs of coffee. He passed one through to Bill and went back to the desk with the other.

'There was another killin' up Tumacacori way,' he said as he savoured the hot drink. 'A Pinkerton agent got hisself knifed while he was checkin' out some fellas who was drivin' a buggy loaded with old clothes and kitchen stuff. Pinkerton's are real keen to get the killer. Offerin' a reward, they be, and I rather fancy I'm the fella what's goin' to collect it. What do you think?'

'I wouldn't know. We didn't travel that route.'

The lawman grinned. 'Is that a fact? Well, I won't argue the point. I've had orders to hold you safe until some military fella gets here. He can identify the men who was with the buggy. Saw them, plain as plain. We're

147

tryin' to sober up Judge Byers right now so that we can have a good hangin' trial. I reckon you're due one, and you're sure worth money to me.'

Bill Hardman tried not to show that he was disturbed.

'What happened to Pete Willet?' he asked. 'Don't he have somethin' to say about this?'

'He lit out, just as I told him. Had all them old clothes bundled across his horse and headin' off for the border. I did notice that he carried a pretty large knife at his belt while you have only an itty bitty thing, but he'd gone before the message came through. That kinda leaves you holdin' the bobcat by the tail, don't it?'

Bill Hardman retired to his bunk to eat the food. He had little hope of Pete ever developing enough courage to try and rescue him from the marshal's clutches. He watched the lawman blowing out the oil-lamps in the office, cursing as his fingers were burned by the hot metal. The place was soon in semi-darkness, only lit by the fitful moon and the slanting rays of light from some building across the street.

'Don't go strolling round the town, fella,' the lawman called cheerfully as he let himself out and turned the large key in the outer door of the jailhouse.

Bill went on eating the beans. The place seemed suddenly quiet and peaceful. If he had not been in danger of a hanging, he would have felt almost at home in the warmth of the little cell. He finished his meal and set the plate down at the side of the bunk. He stretched out to try and get some sleep while the tarantula crawled down the wall a little further to catch a smaller spider that was making a web on the adobe surface.

It was not the noise of the gravel that woke Bill Hardman. It was the stinging of his face as some of the sharp grit hit him on the lips and eyelids. He got up with a start and stared up at the paler gap that indicated the little window. There was a shadow there. A man's head was filling the space and a hand was thrust between the rusty bars.

'Who the hell is that?' Bill shouted in an agitated voice.

'Keep your noise down, fella,' somebody called back. 'I ain't aimin' to be locked up there with you. It's me. Pete.'

Bill Hardman jumped up on the bunk to be closer to the window. It was still above his head and all he could see was the hand that held a few bits of gravel.

'I'm right glad you're here, Pete,' he said gratefully. 'The marshal told me you'd left town.'

He heard the little man laugh. 'That's what he ordered me to do, and I ain't one to argue with the law. But I'm camped down by Taranga Creek. It's ten miles south-west of here and used to be a minin' place. You can't miss it; some huts fallin' apart and a couple of corrals all growed over with cactus.'

'There's just one problem, Pete. How in hell do I get there?'

'Well, I got my shotgun with me. You

figure you could shoot that there lawman and get yo'self a horse?'

'He always comes in with his deputy, and I'd have to have the cell door open before I could do anything. Besides, there ain't no place to hide a shotgun in here. Have you got a pistol?'

'No. You know I ain't. Never did want to own one in case some fella thought that I could use it. I got me a knife.'

Bill grunted. 'I know all about that, Pete,' he said drily. 'That's one of my problems right now. Have you any money on you?'

'Two or three dollars. I bin relyin' on you for money.'

'We can't afford to buy a pistol then, even if you could get one in this town. I only got fifteen dollars left to my name. Look, Pete, you gotta watch out for Helen McCourt and whoever she brings into town with her. She's dangerous. Then there's an army fella comin' to identify me as bein' in company with that crooked Pinkerton agent. I got real troubles here. Do you think these bars will pull out?'

He could hear Pete snorting his answer. 'These walls is thick and the bars is set firm. You're in that cell until somebody turns the key,' he growled. Then there was a long silence before the little man spoke again.

'Bill,' he said in a hesitant fashion, 'I got news about Helen McCourt. She's already here in town with the other Morland brother.'

Bill Hardman thought about it for a moment.

'Has she seen the marshal?' he asked.

'That's the strange part,' Pete Willet answered. 'She's stayin' at the hotel across the way from the jailhouse, but she just ain't showin' herself around. What do you reckon to it?'

'I don't know. Keep out of her way. There's no point both of us bein' in trouble. Is Jesse's money safe?'

'Safe as in a bank. It's still in the kettle at my campsite. I buried it there until I get back. What can we do, Bill?'

The prisoner shook his head. 'I don't know,' he admitted, 'but I sure figured on Helen McCourt rushin' to the marshal and tryin' to get her hands on everythin' he's taken off me and shoved in that next cell. Lookit, Pete, the best thing you can do is to get out of town and deliver that money to Jesse. I'll just have to sort this out for myself. Get going, fella, and good luck to you.'

They spoke for a few minutes longer, and then the little man lowered himself into the saddle of his patient horse and quietly left the scene. Bill Hardman climbed off the bunk and lay down to get some sleep.

The marshal appeared at his usual time the next morning. With the deputy standing guard, he brought Bill Hardman some breakfast and then locked the cell again to go and sit at his desk, drinking coffee and playing patience. The deputy had left to patrol the town and the jailhouse was silent except for the snapping of the pasteboards and the tick of a wall clock.

The sudden opening of the door woke Bill Hardman from a light doze. He sat up to see a man and a woman enter the office. The marshal rose from his chair to greet them and his bulk was momentarily imposed between Bill and the visitors. It was only when he backed up towards the cell door that the prisoner could see the two guns that were pointed at the lawman.

TWELVE

'What the hell...!' the marshal shouted angrily as he was forced against the bars of Bill Hardman's cell. 'You can't come walkin' into my town and holdin' up the jailhouse.'

The woman waved her gun at him impatiently. She moved to within a couple of feet of the bewildered man and pointed the weapon at his large belly.

'We've come for the money you got off this fella,' she said bleakly.

He stared at her in complete puzzlement and then turned to look at Bill Hardman.

'What money?' the marshal asked.

Helen McCourt pressed the barrel of the gun into his flesh. 'You took a packet of money from this killin' bastard and chased Pete Willet outa town,' she said tersely. 'I want that money and I aim to get it. Phil here is good at makin' people talk and he's right angry just now. Two of his brothers have been killed and he ain't aimin' to leave this town without shown' a profit.'

'A profit,' the large man with her repeated dully. He was as big as the marshal but with a reddish face that was pock-marked and had a slightly vacant look.

'I don't know anythin' about any money,' the lawman protested angrily. 'All this fella had on him was fifteen dollars. Who the hell are you, anyhow?'

'It's Helen McCourt,' Bill Hardman said cheerfully. 'She ain't the law-abidin' citizen you imagined, Marshal. She's sure goin' to get that money you took.'

The lawman swung round to face the prisoner. 'I didn't take no money,' he almost whined. 'You never had more than fifteen dollars and it's still in your pocket. Show her, for God's sake!'

Bill Hardman was beginning to see some sense in what was happening. The fact that she knew about Pete Willet meant that he must have contacted her. He must also have fed her the story about the marshal getting Jesse's money. Pete appeared to have made an effort to give his friend a fighting chance. Bill had to make the most of it.

'You've won, Helen,' he said sadly. 'This marshal fella is one clever operator. He sussed me out as soon as he saw me. Pete lit out fast as fast. He knew the game was up.'

'Get me that packet or I'll blow your head off,' Helen McCourt said as she poked the lawman in the ribs with the gun. 'We ain't got all day, fella.'

The marshal plucked up some courage as

he got over the first shock.

'You start shootin' around here, lady,' he said, 'and my deputy's gonna come bustin' in with a few of the townfolk. You're stymied, and well you know it.'

The big man at Helen's side let out a chuckle. 'I done killed your deputy,' he said proudly. 'Clean broke his neck I did. That right, Helen?'

'You sure did, Phil, and the locals ain't goin' to butt in if they don't know what it's all about. Folk is mighty scared of bein' mixed up in a gunfight. So just stop jawin' and hand over my money.'

The marshal was backed tightly against the bars of the cell with Helen's gun still poking him in his ample stomach. The butt of his own Colt was pressed against the cell door, hidden from view but within reach of the prisoner's hand. Bill reached out and quietly slipped it from the holster.

Nobody had noticed his move, but as he pulled back the hammer, the noise it made caused the other three to suddenly take an interest in the man they thought was safely behind bars and without weapons. Phil reacted slowly. His brain seemed to work on half speed. Before he could decide what to do, Bill Hardman pulled the trigger and the shot took the big man in the centre of the chest.

He spun round slightly, tried to raise his own gun, but staggered against the wall and slowly sank down with a long smear of blood streaking the woodwork.

The marshal needed no more help. He swung his right arm against the barrel of Helen's gun and knocked her hand aside as she pulled the trigger. Her shot struck one of the iron bars and fell as a flattened lump of lead to the floor of the cell. Before she could get off another shot, the lawman had her gun by the barrel and was wrenching it out of her hand. She staggered for a moment and then dropped it to run for the door.

He levelled the pistol at her fleeing figure and then angrily lowered it.

He looked at Bill Hardman and shrugged. 'Damn it to hell,' he muttered, 'I can't shoot a woman.'

'I know how you feel, Marshal.' The young man grinned as he returned the lawman's own gun to him. 'But she's as dangerous a hellcat as you'll ever meet.'

The marshal nodded a reluctant agreement, shoved his Colt back in the holster and went over to the desk. He opened a drawer and took out his keys. Without saying a word, he unlocked the cell and Bill Hardman stepped free.

The marshal put the keys back in the desk and took Bill's holster and gun from the rack in the far corner of the office.

'I reckon as how I owe you for savin' my life back there,' he said as he passed them across. 'You got some explainin' to do, but I don't figure the McCourt woman will be filin' charges against you for stealin' her rig. I'm sure that Pete Willet killed the Pinkerton man. Sorta thing a little cuss like him would do. You can leave town any time you like, but right now I'd appreciate a little help in lookin' for my deputy.'

Bill told the marshal as much as he thought wise to disclose, and then the two men left the office to make a search. They found the deputy a few minutes later. He was behind one of the stores and his neck had been broken as though by a single powerful blow.

The town was searched without success for the fleeing Helen McCourt. A few people claimed to have seen her shockingly astride a horse, galloping off to the south-west and trailing a cloud of dust. There was no sign of Pete Willet and the marshal was quite happy for Bill to go on his way. The buggy was left behind, along with Helen's old Navy Colt, but all Bill's gear was returned to him and he was able to ride off to see if Pete was still camped at Taranga Creek.

He kept a sharp look-out as he travelled, glancing around every few minutes in case Helen McCourt was trailing behind. The day was clear and hot, with the dry taste of dust in the air and the drone of myriad insects. The mountains stood out clearly in the distance with trees round their bases and a hint of snow on their peaks.

Bill was worried. Anything could have happened to Pete and he was beginning to feel quite attached to the timid little man who had at least plucked up enough courage to think of a trick that might open the door of the jailhouse. He was not quite sure where Taranga Creek lay, but the trail was heading south-west and if it had once been a mining centre, then it would lie on the main route.

Bill found a small stream after a while and let his horse rest and water. There were no grazing cattle in sight and no signs of human habitation as he started off again. He kept to the same worn trail that looked little-used and was beginning to get overgrown. He was still watching out sharply in case Helen McCourt was following him, but it was not the young woman who suddenly appeared over a ridge to the west.

It was a troop of cavalry.

THIRTEEN

Bill Hardman reined in his horse and waited for them to approach. There was no point in doing anything else. He had nothing to hide and he could not outrun a troop of cavalry who were used to hard riding. He had enough experience of questioning people to know how the officer in charge would act. It was just a matter of staying calm and telling a reasonable story. They could search him without causing any problems and then would have to let him go on his way.

The patrol was led by a young, fresh-faced officer who wore the single bars of a lieutenant. He gave a salute and Bill nodded in return.

'Where would you be heading, sir?' the young man asked politely.

Bill waved a vague hand in the direction of

Mexico. 'I'm huntin' someone, Lieutenant,' he said in an official voice. 'Actin' as deputy for Marshal Sloan of Wryton. You may have heard about the shootin' back there?'

The officer shook his head and eyed the old marshal's badge which Bill had pulled from his pocket to wave at the army man.

'Can't say I have,' he said. 'We ain't been patrolling in that area.'

'Well, a woman by the name of McCourt killed a deputy and tried to shoot the marshal. Her partner was dealt with but she escaped headin' in this direction. She's one dangerous creature.'

'We certainly ain't sighted her,' the officer said. 'You're the first rider we've come across since we set out on patrol today. Why in hell should a female go shooting up a lawman? She sounds loco.'

Bill Hardman gave what he hoped was a discreet smile.

'I reckon it was somethin' personal between her and Marshal Sloan,' he said with a slight wink. 'He was sure hoppin' mad about it.'

The sergeant at the officer's side gave vent to a chuckle that subsided when his superior looked at him.

'Well, I reckon we won't keep you from your chores,' the lieutenant said, 'but we gotta make a search of everybody we meet along the border. I take it you got no objection to that?'

Bill shrugged. 'None at all,' he said easily. 'I heard tell of the killin' of Colonel Barstin's wife from Marshal Sloan. I reckon as how you have a job to do, Lieutenant.'

The search of his person and saddle-bags was soon over and the officer saluted again before leading his troop away at a steady canter towards the east. Bill Hardman watched them go with a feeling of relief before heading once more for Taranga Creek.

He had gone about a mile when he heard the sound of a horse in the distance. It was coming from the east; a cavalry trooper was riding towards him and waving a gauntleted hand for him to stop.

As the rider got nearer, Bill could see the dusty sergeant's stripes and waited impatiently for the man to catch up. The rider pulled rein with enough tautness to set his horse back on its hind legs. He beat his hat against a dusty knee and filled the air with a reddish cloud. The sweat stood out on his heated face as he gave Bill Hardman a broad grin.

'That young whippersnapper fella forgot to tell you,' he said cheerfully, 'but we're lookin' for another killer as well as them what shot the colonel's wife. There's a little runt of about fifty who looks like a drowned gopher, so they tell me. He stabbed a Pinkerton man up near Tumacacori. He ain't got far yet, but the Pinkerton fella's Indian scouts spotted him and he was headin' for the border. He's armed with a shotgun as well as a knife, so watch out for him. I reckon there's a reward to be picked up there.'

'Thanks for tellin' me, Sergeant,' Bill said with a straight face. 'I'll certainly be lookin' out for him.'

The man nodded and turned his horse to gallop off again. Bill Hardman allowed himself to smile a little but did not move until the sergeant was out of sight and could not see the direction in which Bill was heading.

Taranga Greek was a narrow and fast-flowing stream that wound through the sparse grassland like a silver thread. There were some wooden huts with roofs that had collapsed, and several adobe buildings that were crumbling under the steady winds from the mountains. Signs of old mine-workings were everywhere, with large spoil heaps of different colours amid broken sluices of rotting timber.

There was no sign of life. It was eerily quiet with hardly a bird among the low trees and clumps of mesquite. Bill sat his horse on the edge of the little place and looked around carefully. The wind-scoured ground told him nothing and there was no sign of a camp-fire.

His right hand rested above the butt of his gun as he rode slowly along the side of the creek with the rows of tumbledown shacks to his right and left. A broken door flapped in the wind for a moment and his fingers dropped to the comforting butt of the Colt. Then a rat scurried across the trail and his horse faltered as it eyed the creature nervously.

It was another animal that broke the silence of the place. He heard the jingle of harness somewhere behind one of the ruined adobe huts. It was at the far end of the little group of buildings and Bill Hardman took the precaution of riding between some of the other cabins so that he could come upon the animal from behind.

It was easy to recognize Pete Willet's horse. It was in a tumbledown corral which contained a wooden trough of water and a few bundles of coarse grass. The animal looked contented enough and barely paid attention to the newcomers. The saddle was draped over the fence but the bit was still in its mouth and it was that which had alerted Bill Hardman.

He sat silently as his eyes moved to cover the small huts and broken-down corrals around him. The natural sounds of the day were all there but there was a total absence of human occupation. The horse had not been in the corral very long. He could tell that by the droppings and the amount of fodder that was piled on the ground. Pete Willet had to be somewhere close by. He could not have moved far without a horse.

'I've been waitin' for you, Hardman.'

It was a woman's voice and Bill turned in the saddle to find himself facing Helen McCourt. She stood in the doorway of a small adobe hut with a shotgun in her hands. It was cocked and pointing at him with a steady aim. The woman's dark hair was covered with a fine layer of dust and her face showed signs of fatigue as she stood in the harsh sunlight. Despite that, her grip on the gun was steady and her face was a hard mask of determination.

'Where's Pete?' It was the only thing that Bill Hardman could think of on the spur of the moment.

She smiled slightly. 'He lit out,' she said. 'I'd have killed the lyin' little coyote if I'd laid eyes on him. He played me one hell of a trick back there in Wryton. I don't reckon as how that marshal had Jesse's poke at all. Am I right?'

Bill nodded. He needed to play for time until he could turn the tables on the woman.

'How'd you know I'd be comin' here?' he asked.

'Easy. I know Jesse Clark's way of doin' things across the border,' she said with a grim smile. 'He's used this place a dozen times or more. Plenty of water, a bit of shelter, and only another few miles to Mexico. I'm not stupid, Mr Hardman. Now, let's stop playin' games. Where's the money?'

'I've passed it on.'

The shotgun moved menacingly in her strong hands.

'You're lying,' she said angrily.

'That's why we went to Wryton. Jesse didn't

trust Pete to carry it, and he knew there were patrols all along the border because of that army wife's killing. So he arranged for somebody to meet us at Wryton.'

'Who?'

Bill shrugged. 'I don't know his name, but he was a black fella,' he said.

The woman frowned as she thought about it.

'A black fella,' she mused. 'One of the Morland boys mentioned a black fella on Jesse's rig. But who the hell is he?'

'I don't know, but he was at Jesse's place in Mexico when I went there. Seemed to be right at home. I figure Jesse reckoned as how no army patrol or lawman would be thinkin' of a black fella carryin' anythin' valuable. He didn't even have a gun at his belt. Just an old shotgun. And he was ridin' a mule. Real poor-looking.'

The woman stood undecided while Bill remained motionless astride his horse.

'Get down from there and empty your saddlebags.'

The order took him by surprise but he hastened to obey. She watched avidly as everything was tumbled on to the sand.

'Now, drop your gunbelt,' she ordered, 'and don't make any mistakes about it. I'm not feelin' any too friendly.'

He did as she ordered and let the gun fall to the ground.

'Now strip.'

Bill's mouth dropped open. 'Lady, you have to be loco!' he protested. 'I've told you I ain't got the money!'

'Strip. I ain't foolin' around, fella, and you ain't got no time for modesty. So get on with it.'

'Look, lady–'

'I can always shoot first and then search what's left of you. Have it whichever way you want.'

Bill Hardman slowly undressed. His tanned face went a deeper shade as he piled his clothes in front of her.

'Satisfied now?' he asked in a small voice.

'I reckon so.'

There was a strange lack of interest in her voice and he suddenly realized that she was not really looking at him but at something that seemed to lie beyond his right shoulder. Bill Hardman turned instinctively and drew a tight breath as he saw the group of horsemen who sat their mounts on a sandy slope at the end of the row of buildings.

They were pueblo Indians. The same ones who had accompanied the crooked Pinkerton agent. And they were within shooting range.

FOURTEEN

'Lady, you are in real trouble.' Bill Hardman turned back to look at the frightened woman.

'You know who they are?' she asked hoarsely.

'I sure do. Pete Willet knifed their boss and

I reckon as how they're on the warpath. A nicely built woman like you would do them a treat.'

Helen McCourt gave vent to an unladylike curse and turned sharply to enter the little hut just behind her. Bill Hardman bent down to pick up his gun but then changed his mind and decided that putting on his pants was more important. As he was dressing, he heard the sound of a horse galloping off at a spanking pace. He caught a glimpse of Helen as she rode towards the west in a flurry of dust in an effort to put as much distance as possible between herself and hostile Indians.

Bill was fastening his gunbelt by the time the group of horsemen surrounded him, sitting silently on their mounts with blank, expressionless faces as they stared at this strange white man who had stood naked only a few moments ago.

'If you're lookin' for Pete,' Bill said in as cheerful a voice as he could muster, 'he lit out long before I got here. Gone over to

173

Mexico, I shouldn't wonder.'

One of the Indians came closer. The sweat from the lips of his horse dripped on Bill Hardman's boots.

'Little man with big knife,' he said in a quiet voice. 'He kill man who pay us. We want our money.'

Bill Hardman breathed a sigh of relief. This was no Indian war party but a group of peaceful folk who just felt that they had been cheated out of their wages. He shook his head sadly and stroked the muzzle of the horse that was slobbering over his feet.

'Well,' he said slowly, 'you saw that woman ridin' out of here hell for leather? She's after him too. He promised to marry her, and then lit out. She's real sore, and it don't help that he's taken some of her money as well. You follow her trail and you might meet up with him. If she don't kill him first.'

The little group discussed something in flat voices before their spokesman turned again to Bill Hardman.

'Why you wear no clothes?' he asked.

'Ah, now that's another story. She thought that I might try and stop her followin' him. Y'see, he owes me money as well, and she don't aim for me to find him before she does. A man don't travel too well until he's dressed again. If you hadn't showed up, she might have taken my clothes with her.'

There was another short discussion and the little group of horsemen was closer and seemed more menacing. Bill Hardman was sweating now and his nervous eye alighted on the solitary horse in the corral.

'I can help you get some of your wages back,' he said with a fine show of sincerity.

'How?'

'Well, that cow pony there and the saddle on the fence belong to the man you're lookin' for. I reckon he made off on foot and can't travel too fast. If he killed your boss, it would be mighty fair to take that pony and the saddle as part payment.'

There was another short bit of talking and a nodding of heads. Bill began to relax a little.

'You good man,' the leader said in his flat voice. 'We follow woman. You go in peace.'

Two of the Indians dismounted and opened the gate of the corral. They soon had the horse and saddle in their possession and headed off towards the west in pursuit of Helen McCourt and Pete Willet. Bill Hardman leaned against the fence with a foolish grin on his face. He was trembling slightly and it took a few minutes for him to start thinking straight again.

He had to find Pete, and the fact that the little man had vanished while leaving his horse and saddle behind was a bad sign. He did not think that Helen had killed him. She would have admitted it quite cheerfully. Either he had fled when he heard her arriving, or someone else had made away with him.

His saddle-bags were missing, as was the iron kettle. There had also been the sacks of used clothes to be accounted for. Bill looked round at the various huts and decided that he would have to search each one.

It did not take very long. All the ruined adobe buildings were empty and did not look as if anybody had used them for years. They made dark and smelly homes for bats, scorpions, and a myriad of spiders. Bill stepped back into the open air with a feeling of relief. He looked around in bewilderment as he listened to the rustling wind and the creaking of ancient woodwork.

'You didn't have to give 'em my horse!'

The voice was reproachful and it came from the flat roof of one of the adobe huts. Bill's hand went automatically towards his gun until he realized that Pete Willet had finally put in an appearance.

The little man's face peered over the edge of the roof and it was clear that he had been hiding behind a low parapet and was able to listen to or see everything that was happening below him.

'You can come down now, Pete,' Bill said with reluctant admiration. 'I've sent them all chasin' their tails.'

He had a few minutes to wait while the

little man climbed down a rickety ladder at the back of the hut and then came round to the front with a wide grin on his dusty face.

'I could sure use some hot coffee,' he said as he licked his parched lips. 'Let's go to where I'm camped and I'll make some.'

Bill Hardman grabbed him by the arm. 'Hold it a minute, Pete,' he said anxiously. 'Is Jesse's money safe?'

'As safe as in a Tucson bank, fella. I'm no lost steer at this sort of thing. Me and Jesse have been workin' together a lotta years. Come on now, and let's eat.'

He led the way past the ruined buildings and down a rocky slope by the stream to a long stand of wind-bent trees that hung over the water and provided shade for a family of jackrabbits. They scuttled off at the sight of the intruders. Pete's camp was behind the trees.

There was nothing to show at first, and it was not until he had cleared some of the bushes that the sacks of used clothes came to light. They lay along with his saddle-bags, blankets, and the old shotgun that was his only weapon, save for the large knife at his belt.

The kettle was there, buried in the sand, and Pete dug it up triumphantly to display with pride as he took off the lid to show the oilskin-wrapped parcel that still lay safely inside.

'I reckon that Jesse owes me on this one,' he said proudly. 'I've never been so scared in all my life. When I heard that McCourt woman gallopin' up, I thought it was you. I got one hell of a shock when I sees her ridin' like some liquored-up Indian, I ran back among the huts to where I was when you arrived. And them Indians didn't help none, either. They're really after my hide. Did you have to give them my horse and saddle?'

Bill grinned. 'I was tryin' to stay alive, Pete. Just like you. How far is it to Jesse's place now?'

'About fifteen miles the way we're going. The border's almost six miles due south and then we can make a pretty straight line to

Jesse's place. The Mexican patrols ain't as keen as our lot. They like a nice rest in the heat of the day, and that's when we'll be travelling.'

'Fair enough. We'll have to ride turn and turn about. These sacks'll have to be left here.'

'And the kettle?'

'We sure as hell take the kettle.'

Both men laughed and Pete began to start a fire while Bill filled the enamel pot and also added water to the iron kettle ready to place it near the flames in case any army patrols came along.

They were soon sitting down with tin plates of food on their knees while the aroma of hot coffee filled the air as they took a welcome meal.

'Suppose you tell me what happened back in Wryton,' Bill said as they ate.

'Well, I didn't see no way of helpin' you get outa jail,' Pete said as he chewed on the fatty bacon, 'and I gotta be honest, fella. I sure thought of gettin' the hell out and startin' a new life some place else. Then the McCourt woman's arrival gave me an idea. A hell of a lot depended on you havin' a chance if I started things moving. You sure as hell took it. I just told her that the marshal had shoved you in the jailhouse and had the money tucked away in his office for his own use. She couldn't wait to go gunnin' for the fella. I had to hope that you'd have a chance while all the shootin' was goin' on.'

'I got my chance,' Bill said quietly, 'and the Morland fella's dead. I reckon our troubles are about over now and we'll have an easy run to Jesse's place.'

'Not so easy if we're takin' it in turns to walk,' Pete said drily. 'I ain't used to doin' things like that.'

'It'll be hard going, but at least the worst is over. Them Indians will keep Helen McCourt on the move.'

Pete looked doubtful.

'I hope you're right. I wouldn't like to meet up with her again. She's one vengeful woman.'

FIFTEEN

Pete Willet and Bill Hardman rode and walked slowly towards the frontier. The heat of the day passed them by as they travelled along shady gullies and between masses of stunted mesquite or other bushes that could be used as cover from the questing eyes of any patrol.

The sun got nearer to the horizon as they crossed a small creek which Pete Willet declared knowingly, was the border between the two countries. They were in Mexican territory now and Bill Hardman felt a certain sense of relief that he was close to finishing the long and wearying job that had cost so many lives.

They turned slightly west, heading between two ranges of steep hills. The going was uneven and they changed from horse to foot at more frequent intervals. Pete was the one who found the going tough. He was not used to hard, physical effort, and his pace became slower as the shadows lengthened across the trail.

They halted eventually for an evening meal. A trickle of pure water ran down between a mass of dark rock and emptied into a narrow creek that flowed into the wide valley ahead of them. Pete lit a fire while Bill unpacked the saddle-bags and spread worn blankets on the ground. The sun had long since vanished and a few stars shone in a cloudless, dark sky. The smell of bacon and beans filled the air as they sat down to enjoy their first meal for hours.

They slept after a while, lulled by the regular sounds of the night. Their solitary horse and the scurrying small creatures were noises that did not intrude as they both snored peacefully under the thin blankets with their heads resting on the saddle-bags.

Bill Hardman was not sure what woke him, but he was instantly alert, his hand reaching automatically for the Colt that lay nearby. He sat up, listening acutely for some unusual sound.

There it was again. A distant shot, followed by another after a slight pause. He stood up and gave Pete a nudge with his foot as he did so. The little man let out a startled yell before recovering his wits and grabbing the shotgun. The two men stood side by side, listening for more firing.

It came almost immediately: a volley that might have been six or seven shots. Even the horse took notice and raised its head in slight alarm.

'Maybe them Indians caught up with Helen McCourt,' Pete Willet murmured hopefully.

'Could be, but there's sure a hell of a lotta shootin' out there.'

This was confirmed almost at once by another volley of shots. The horse moved uneasily and pulled at its tether.

'How far away would you say it was?' Bill asked quietly.

'A mile perhaps, or less. You ain't thinkin' of joinin' in, are you?'

'Not to save Helen McCourt, but there's a friend of mine out there somewhere, and I don't aim that he should get into trouble on her account. You stay here and keep the fire goin' while I take a look at what's happenin' out there. After all, Pete, we have to travel in that direction in the morning. I'd like to think we weren't headin' into some sort of trap.'

The little man considered it for a moment and then nodded dubious agreement.

Bill Hardman saddled the horse and set out in the direction from which the shots had come. The moon was rising and the sky was still cloudless. It was easy enough to see the trail and his sure-footed mount made a steady pace through the chill of the night. As he rode, several more explosions tore the air, and when he finally breasted a rise to view the terrain ahead, he could see flashes amid a grove of trees that clustered round a creek.

The gunfire was sporadic now, and there were faint shouts in Spanish. As Bill watched from the top of the slope, it was possible to see the mounted Mexican army patrol galloping round a small defended position and trying to break in. It was a group of Indians who had been trapped and they were trying to reach their horses while at the same time defending themselves from their enemy.

They were the pueblo Indians who had been hunting Pete and Helen McCourt. Bill Hardman breathed a sigh of relief that what was happening did not concern him. He turned to ride back to his own camp just as the patrol finally broke through the volley of rifle fire and clashed with the scattering Indians.

Some of them reached their ponies and fled wildly away from the scene. They galloped north again, passing within a couple of hundred yards of Bill while he watched in fascination. The Mexicans ignored them to concentrate on the ones who were still on foot.

Bill quietly left the scene before anybody noticed him and rode back to camp at a steady pace.

Pete Willet had kicked the fire alight again and the enamel coffee-pot was bubbling away above it. Bill looked round, thinking that the little man had gone into hiding at all the noise of passing horses and continuous yelling mingled with gunshots. Bill called his name as he climbed out of the saddle and tethered his horse to a tree.

There was no reply, and he called again. His voice only disturbed a few birds and some creature that scuttled across his feet. It was then that he saw the blood. It was illuminated by the flickering light of the fire. There was a trail of it and it led to a clump of mesquite where Pete Willet lay on his back with a smashed skull.

There was also a vivid gash across his throat and his shotgun and boots were missing.

There was nothing that Bill could do. The

fleeing Indians had caught up with the man who had deprived them of their wages. As they fled the Mexican patrol, the light of Pete's fire had led them straight to him. Bill left the body where it was and went back to take the enamel pot off the flames. It was then that he realized that the blankets and saddle-bags were missing. The Indians had slopped long enough to take everything they could.

He heard a yell in the distance and looked up at the long ridge to the north. Three of the Indians sat their horses there, waving defiance to Mexico and waving something else that could be clearly seen in the bright moonlight.

It was a large iron kettle.

SIXTEEN

Bill Hardman followed the trail that Pete had mapped out and came in sight of Jesse Clark's hideaway just after dawn broke with a faint mist lifting from the ground. He had ridden carefully, always on the watch for patrols as he steered his mount over the uneven terrain.

Jesse's money was safe. He had been wary enough to remove it from the kettle when he left Pete at the campsite. Bill had felt that with all the danger appearing to be over, and Jesse's home only a few miles away, Pete might try some trick either on his own account or on Jesse's orders.

He felt guilty at having mistrusted him now and shivered in the chill air at the thought of the body he had left behind by the dead camp-fire.

By the time he breasted the rise and rode down towards the little farmhouse, the sun was warming up the ground and the birds were twittering happily as they searched for their early morning food. Smoke drifted from the chimney of the small adobe building and, as Bill neared it, the dark figure of Sam appeared in the doorway with a shotgun at the ready.

He grinned when he saw who the visitor was and lowered the weapon. Bill noticed that another gun had been covering him from one of the windows and he could see the large outline of Jesse Clark through the glass. He dismounted and loosened the girth of his mount. The black man leaned the shotgun against the wall and took charge of the horse while Bill walked across to the open door to be greeted by a smiling Jesse.

'You're a welcome sight for sore eyes, lad,' the man said jovially as he shook hands. 'Where's Pete? Didn't you pick him up?'

Bill explained what had happened while

Sam made coffee and poured it out. Jesse listened with a frown on his stout face. He shook his head in sorrow and was silent for a moment when the story ended. Then he suddenly bucked up as if the mourning had passed and been forgotten.

'And my money?' he asked eagerly.

Bill produced the sealed packet and handed it over. Jesse drew an audible sigh of relief as he inspected the precious object.

'You've done well, fella,' he said warmly. He got up from the table to open an old salt box on the wall and extract a bundle of money. He counted out $500 and handed it to Bill.

'We won't knock off the fifty dollars I sent you,' he said. 'You earned every cent of it. It's a shame about Pete. You were right not to trust him. He was no angel, but I shall miss him.'

He sat down again, sighed heavily and then drank some of the scalding coffee.

'Now, will you be staying the night and setting off again when you've rested up?' he asked solicitously.

Bill rose from his chair and held out a hand.

'No, Mr Clark. If it's all the same with you, I'll be off to make the best of the daylight hours. I'm glad you're satisfied and I'm real sorry about Pete. I kinda liked the little fella. He weren't quite the coward he thought he was.'

Jesse nodded sadly as he showed his guest to the door. Sam had already gone to saddle the horse and he and Jesse watched as their visitor mounted and rode out of the farm area. The sun was high now and there was a buzzing of insects in the air.

Bill rode along contentedly at first, but after he had gone about half a mile, a nagging thought began to creep into his mind. He reined in the horse, sat restlessly for a few minutes under the hot sun, and then turned back towards the farm.

He halted before the building came into sight, tethered his mount, and went forward on foot. There was no sign of Sam or any farm worker around the outside of the house, and Bill was able to get close without being observed. He removed his spurs and crept silently to peer into the window of the room where he and Jesse had talked.

The fat man was seated at the table with the opened packet in front of him. He had the contents in his hands and held them up to the light to appreciate fully the sparkle of the emeralds in their gold settings.

His face went a chalky white when the door burst open and framed a furious Bill Hardman who stood, gun in hand, like some avenging angel.

'What in hell are you doing back here?' Jesse Clark gulped in a panic-stricken voice. He started to rise from the table while at the same time thrusting the jewellery into his pocket.

Bill stepped forward and waved the gun for him to sit down again.

'I opened that package,' he said quietly, 'just to make sure that I was only carryin' money. Then I sealed it up again. When you looked it over a few minutes ago, you didn't spot the poor job I'd done on it. So I figured that it was a different packet. Pete Willet switched them. Am I right?'

Jesse Clark was recovering from the shock.

'Quite right, lad,' he said cheerfully. 'I arranged to buy this necklace but I needed the money I'd left back in Santa Rosa. So you were engaged to get it for me, and when you arrived in Wryton, Pete was to meet those who held up the carriage and swap packages. A simple business deal.'

'I sure as hell was one prize donkey,' Bill said bitterly.

'Well, maybe you were, but you were well paid, and that's what it's all about. Look now, I'll give you another two hundred dollars and you can be on your way. No hard feelings. Eh?'

'You haven't got enough money to cover this one, Clark.'

The fat man smiled. His confidence was now so complete that Bill felt a twinge of anxiety.

'I'm handin' you and this necklace over to

the law,' he said in what he hoped was a determined voice.

'No, son. You're doing no such thing. Y'see, Sam is right behind you and he's got a shotgun in the small of your back. Now, I'm loyal to them as is loyal to me, so I reckon you should leave now.'

Bill Hardman glanced over his shoulder. The black man stood just behind him, his eyes wide and scared. But he held the gun firmly and its twin barrels were within inches of their target.

'You do what the boss tells you, fella,' Sam said in a slightly edgy voice. 'You got no more business here now.'

Bill Hardman held his ground. 'You're in trouble, Jesse,' he said firmly. 'There are Pinkerton men right here in Mexico, and they know I was carryin' somethin' for you. They'll hunt you down for the reward, and your life won't mean a thing to them. Tell Sam to put the gun away.'

Jesse laughed. 'Ignore him, Sam. He's scared.'

'Jesse,' Bill pleaded, 'two women were killed for that necklace. Ma Barstin and her servant girl. You were in on it, and that's somethin' you'll have to live with. A lotta people got reason to hunt you down.'

Jesse Clark waved a chubby hand dismissively.

'A crooked woman who robbed her own family, and a no-account black girl! What in hell do they matter? When I planned that hold-up, fella, I didn't intend for anyone to be killed, but what does it signify? These things happen. It's over and done with, and so are you. Take him outside and kill him, Sam.'

'I ain't killin' nobody,' the black man said with fierce dignity. 'If you was the one as brought about the deaths of them women, then you're the one I should be shooting. But you saved my life, and I can't forget that. So I'm quitting. You and this fella can fight your own battles.'

Jesse Clark reached out a pleading hand. 'Don't leave, Sam,' he shouted. 'This fella will kill me. Stay here, lad. You've got a home with me.'

The black man propped the shotgun against the wall and turned on his heel. Jesse was left facing the steadily held Colt that now controlled the situation.

Bill Hardman left the farm a short time later. He mounted his horse and headed back the way he had come. He stopped after a few hundred yards to throw the shotgun into a patch of cactus before turning towards a large clump of mesquite over on his right. He drew rein in front of it and placed a hand on the butt of his gun as he leaned forward in the saddle.

'I delivered the package, Miss McCourt,' he said quietly. 'Jesse got what he was expecting.'

There was a rustle among the flowering bushes and a slight haze of dust fell from the leaves.

'How did you know I was here?' she asked angrily.

Bill grinned. 'If I'd been in your boots, lady,' he said, 'this is where I'd have come. And I seen the trail your pony left when you headed into the mesquite. You and Jesse can settle things now. I've been paid.'

'Where's Pete?'

'Indians killed him. They figured they had a right to.'

There was a moment of silence before she spoke again.

'I could kill you right here and now for all the trouble you've given me,' she said bitterly.

'But you won't, lady. A shot would warn Jesse, and that wouldn't do, would it? And you couldn't kill me when I was ridin' in, because you didn't know where Pete was. He might have been watchin' my back.'

Bill moved on, a hand still hovering above the butt of the Colt in case she got any ideas about the money he was carrying. He could hear the movements of her horse among the bushes as she turned it angrily towards the farm. He stopped to watch her ride down the slope and leap from her mount at the door of the building. There was a gun in her hand and she was ready to use it.

Bill Hardman had not bothered to tell her that while he had taken Jesse's shotgun, he had not removed the fat man's Colt .44. All that Bill had done was to unload it and scatter the bullets around the floor. It was all he needed to give himself time to be out of firing range. He reckoned that Jesse would have the weapon reloaded by now.

A shot came from the adobe house, quickly followed by another one. Then there was a silence. Bill waited to see if anyone emerged. Nobody did and he rode back to the building and dismounted at the hitching rail.

The door was still open and a slight haze of acrid smoke hung in the air. Jesse Clark lay by the table, his hand still holding the gun as he twitched out his life. Helen McCourt was dead. Jesse's shot had taken her in the middle of the forehead.

The dying man looked at Bill Hardman

with hatred in his fading eyes.

'You ruined everything,' he muttered as he raised the pistol and tried to pull back the hammer. The effort was too much and it slipped from his fingers.

Bill rode briskly along the trail to the north and made camp for the night in the same place that he had used on his first visit to Jesse Clark's hideout. He had a reason for halting there. It was where he had encountered Bert Ebdon, the Pinkerton agent. With a fire lit and the smell of coffee, the man might appear again, coming out of the darkness this time in what could be hoped to be a more friendly fashion.

Bill made enough coffee for two and put some bacon in the skillet to fill the night air with its strong aroma. He listened for sounds beyond the circle of firelight and was not surprised when the jingle of harness intruded on the other noises of the dark.

'I hope you've brought your own mug, Bert,' he said without turning round. 'Some

Indian fellas stole all my gear, save what was in the saddle-bags.'

'Indians! Where the hell do you get Indians in this part of the country?' Bert Ebdon exclaimed as he tethered his mount and came across to the light and warmth of the fire.

'It's a long story. They was chasin' Pete Willet.'

'Pete Willet? Ain't that the fella employed by Jesse Clark?'

'That's the man. He did somethin' the pueblo Indians didn't like, so they hunted him down, killed the little fella, and stole most of our gear.'

Bert Ebdon passed across the tin plate and enamel mug that he had unpacked.

'I seen you visitin' Jesse's place,' he said quietly.

'I thought you might be watching.'

Bill poured the coffee and piled the man's plate with bacon and beans. Bert Ebdon produced some Mexican bread and the two men began eating in companionable silence.

'You got Jesse's money, then?' Bert asked in a casual voice.

'Yep, and I checked to make sure it was money.'

Bert gave vent to a deep groan of disappointment.

'So I've been wastin' my time sittin' out here gettin' bitten by every crawlin' and flyin' critter they got in this damned country?'

'I reckon so.'

'I was so sure that Jesse Clark was behind that robbery,' Bert Ebdon said bitterly. 'I had him figured for the fella what planned it all.'

He sighed again and took a sip of coffee.

'Jesse must be one happy man right now,' he said savagely.

Bill shook his head. 'Not really,' he said. 'His girlfriend caught up with him and there was a shoot-out. They both lost.'

'Is that a fact, now?'

Bert Ebdon poured himself more coffee and was just raising the mug to his lips when a thought occured to him.

'So who got the money?' he asked sharply.

Bill shrugged. 'Jesse had a black fella workin' for him. I figure as how he's on his way south by now. The richest black fella in Mexico.'

'Hell and damnation. I saw him leave the place.'

The Pinkerton man threw the coffee away angrily.

'I spend all my life waitin' for the big one to come along, and some no-good servant beats me to it. I'm gettin' too old for this, Bill. Much too old. I was bankin' on that money for my old age. A safe roof over my head, a saloon down the street, and stores with all the fripperies a man could want. I went to sleep every night out here, knowin' that it was just a hoot and a holler away. Life sure lets you down.'

'It sure does. It was a mighty big reward.'

Bert Ebdon snorted angrily.

'Reward nothing?' he snapped. 'I was goin' to have the lot, Bill. I can tell you that now. I sat out here and dreamed about it. After all the years I've served the law, what in hell have I got to show for it? Nothin' but achin' bones and nowhere to lay my head when Pinkerton's get rid of me for a younger fella.'

'You were goin' to steal the emeralds instead of just claimin' the reward?' Bill asked in astonishment.

'I sure as hell was.' Bert chuckled bitterly. 'And then I was goin' to live in some big town with no more money worries. So I'd have turned out bad, but that's what poverty does for you, Bill. Well, I can stop dreamin' now and retire an honest man.'

'I guess so.'

Bill Hardman had intended to share the reward for the emeralds that he was carrying. He could now change his mind with a clear conscience and claim it all for himself.

The publishers hope that this book has given you enjoyable reading. Large Print Books are especially designed to be as easy to see and hold as possible. If you wish a complete list of our books please ask at your local library or write directly to:

Dales Large Print Books
Magna House, Long Preston,
Skipton, North Yorkshire.
BD23 4ND